the abc's of
kissing boys

the
abc's
of
kissing
boys

a novel by
Tina
Ferraro

Delacorte Press

Published by Delacorte Press
an imprint of Random House Children's Books
a division of Random House, Inc.
New York

Delacorte Press and colophon are registered trademarks of Random House, Inc.

Visit us on the Web! www.randomhouse.com/teens

Educators and librarians, for a variety of teaching tools, visit us at
www.randomhouse.com/teachers

Library of Congress Cataloging-in-Publication Data
Ferraro, Tina.
The ABC's of kissing boys / Tina Ferraro. — 1st trade paperback ed.
p. cm.
Summary: When sixteen-year-old Parker Stanhope takes kissing lessons from the freshman across the street as part of her plan to get on the varsity soccer team, a relationship blossoms that threatens her popularity at school and must be kept secret from their feuding fathers.
ISBN 978-0-385-73582-7 (tr pbk)—ISBN 978-0-385-90569-5 (glb)
[1. Popularity—Fiction. 2. Interpersonal relations—Fiction. 3. Soccer—Fiction. 4. Neighbors—Fiction. 5. High schools—Fiction. 6. Schools—Fiction. 7. Kissing—Fiction.] I. Title.
PZ7.F365Abc 2009
[Fic]—dc22
2007051601

Printed in the United States of America

The text of this book is set in 12.5-point Filosofia.
Book design by Angela Carlino

10 9 8 7 6 5 4 3 2 1

First Edition

Special thanks to

my incomparable editor, Krista Marino;
my agent, Nadia Cornier, who wouldn't let me quit this book;
author Kelly Parra, for her "cyber fairy dust";
the Buzz Girls, at www.booksboysbuzz.com;
my daughter, Sarah, for her assurances;

my soccer professionals, Bjorn, Stefan and Ashley;

and friends and family who continue to light my way,
including Stacy Gustafson, Paddy Lock, Patricia Mills, Tom,
Heather, Billie, Joe, Russ, Mary and Annie, and the guys who
keep our home fires burning.

For Terri,
'cause she's cool like that

Adrenaline: Senses become engaged when kissing takes place—feeling, seeing, hearing, smelling, tasting. Adrenaline intensifies it all.

"You're late."

Luke was right, and I knew I should apologize. But the reason for this meeting was so embarrassing that the only way I could keep what remained of my pride was to look my brother's friend in the eye and give him attitude right back.

"Yeah, well, *you* try riding in DeGroot traffic on that old thing," I said, and pointed through the music store's front window at my ten-speed bike on the sidewalk. The tires were low and the seat was mostly duct tape, but Luke lived and worked by the university now, and I'd had to get here somehow.

"Me on *that*?" he said, and frowned. "Not a chance."

"Yeah, yeah, Mr. Cool," I said, but added a smile to soften my words. I was, after all, here to get him to do me a favor.

Luke Anderson, last spring's prom king and still the object of most every girl's desire at DeGroot High School, leaned a hip against a display case and shrugged. I'd practically grown up around him, was used to his shrugs and this brother-sister-type bantering. I was also used to him being fairly obsessed with himself and everything Luke-related, so was pleasantly surprised when he agreed to this meeting today. I was starting to get why Clayton had stayed so tight with him all these years.

"Look, Parker," he said, then glanced at the store's wall clock, "I don't have much time, so let's get down to business."

I plunked my scratched-up bike helmet on the counter and ran a hand through my bangs to get them out of my eyes. My hair was so blond that any sweat whatsoever made it look what some called carelessly tousled and what I called an absolute mess. I dug into the pockets of my shorts, came up with a bunch of bills and coins and dumped them unceremoniously into Luke's cupped hands. "Two hundred eighty-six and fourteen cents. It's every penny I have in the world."

He stared down at the cold, hard cash. "That's a really random number."

I saw his point. "Okay, keep two hundred and fifty and give me back the rest."

He frowned, and little lines fanned out from his brown eyes. "I owe your bro some bucks. I'll throw that in and make it an even three hundred. Hartley can't refuse *that*, can she?"

Hartley was Coach Wanda Hartley, or *Heartless*, to me, since she'd posted the soccer rosters two weeks ago and moved up every eleventh-grade player—except two. Hard to believe (and even harder to swallow), but my name, Parker Stanhope, had appeared for the third consecutive year on the JV roster. Alongside those of dull-as-dirt junior Lyric Wolensky, freshmen and other soccer newbies.

After remembering how to breathe, I'd tried to talk to Hartley, to reason with her about her obvious slip in judgment. I mean, how could she expect me to wave goodbye to my friends, to my *life*? Or what was *supposed* to be my life. But she hadn't budged, had just talked about player limits and told me to report to JV practice following the first day of school.

So for now, I was in limbo—a junior on a JV team. Which horrified and humiliated me. And did strange things to my best friends and former teammates Chrissandra Hickey, Elaine Chu and Mandy Kline, too. While full of hugs and *awww*s at first, suddenly they seemed busy now when I called or IM'd. Like I was an illegal alien in their world and they were reconsidering my visa.

All I could think was they were waiting things out, trusting that I'd triumph over this injustice, that I'd make this awkwardness of what to say to me and what not to say go away. But in the still of the night, I couldn't help worrying that they were waiting for *me* to go away. That they were all varsity cool now—and I was not. Which dug like a stake in my heart.

Making things right between my friends and me was the driving force behind this crazy scheme that I had concocted with my brother and that Clayton had gotten Luke to agree to.

School started on a Monday, and the following Tuesday, classes let out at noon for the customary campus sports fair. There was your basic DJ and yummy food booths, and a raffle to give away T-shirts and homework passes and the chance to be principal for a day (like being a student at DHS wasn't lame enough). But the big draw was that each sports team hosted a booth, and the coach of the booth that raised the most money got to park in a very coveted reserved teacher parking space for the whole school year.

JV soccer always did a milk-bottle ring toss, and varsity soccer went with a kissing booth. This year's kissing booth would go down in history, if Clayton, Luke and I had anything to do with it.

The plan was for Luke and Clayton to be back from the university, presumably to see old friends and teachers. After some schmoozing, Luke would strut up to the three-dollar kissing booth and announce that he was willing to make a very large donation.

For a kiss from me.

When he was told he'd have to choose another girl

because I hadn't made varsity, he would get loud and get demanding—in a charming way. And when you look like a rock star, and the girls at the school are still in love with you, and the guys still want to *be* you, well, you get noticed. And, usually, what you want.

At that point, he'd call on Coach Hartley and tell her if she'd put me on varsity for a few minutes, he'd plunk down what we had now decided would be three hundred dollars. Which we hoped she'd eagerly interpret as a *lock* on that reserved parking spot, the one the teachers called the "sleep in and slip in," because the driver could arrive as late as first bell, park, and still be in class on time.

Clayton, who was just starting his second year at the university and had an eye toward law school, swore that those few minutes I spent on varsity would be enough to substantiate a claim to make Heartless keep me on permanently. Sort of like squatter's rights, he'd said. And having to kick someone off varsity to create the opening (like senior Rachael Washington, whose interest in soccer flip-flopped, anyway, and whose return to the game this year was basically the reason my life seriously sucked) was not too high a price to pay to keep my claim from going to court.

We'd have Heartless by the throat. And I'd have my old life back. Friends and all.

"Thanks," I told Luke, to the offer of padding my money out to three hundred and, well, doing this whole thing for me. "I won't forget this."

"Clayton's saved my butt more times than I can count. I'm glad to help. But one thing," he said, and tilted his head down toward me. "When I go to kiss you, it's gotta look like the real deal. Like I'm enjoying it and getting my money's worth."

Oh, God, there was no denying the majorly masculine look to his eyes.

Heat rose to my face. Not because I was excited about kissing Luke—or repulsed. The truth was, when I looked at him objectively, I saw his hottieness. (A whole town of girls could not be wrong.) But if it weren't for this kissing booth, I would go my entire life without locking lips with him, and that would be just fine, too.

What was making my freckled face blush was his underlying meaning—my inexperience with kissing. Which, in my own defense, was not totally my fault, since I'd had a boyfriend most of my sophomore year. But he'd lived in another part of Minnesota—in my grandmother's town—and had only given me quick, closed-mouth kisses when we'd been alone.

So it's not like I was some prude who was afraid to smear her lip gloss or something. Still, I was as new at kissing as most of the JV soccer team was at high school sports.

"I'm going to give it my all," he went on, taking a step away from the display case and closer to me. "And you're going to have to give it back just as good."

I swallowed. Hard. I couldn't tell if he was joking or strangely serious.

"In fact, when we're done, I expect applause and

whistles. Otherwise, Coach Hartley could catch on that this was all a setup. Then, even if Clayton could somehow get a lawsuit going, she'd fight it every step of the way and make your life frigging miserable.

"And, worse? I'll look stupid." He narrowed his brown eyes at my blue ones. "And Parker, I don't *do* stupid."

I winced, wanting to assure him that I wouldn't botch the kiss. But with nothing in my background to back it up, the words sort of clogged in my throat.

"So do us both a favor," he said, pulling a ten back out from his pocket and handing it to me. "Stop by the supermarket on your way home and pick up some bing cherries and Starburst. I had this girlfriend once who swore she owed her technique to looping cherry stems and unwrapping Starbursts with her tongue."

I'm pretty sure I grimaced.

"Try it. And anything else you can think to help get you up to par." He glanced at the clock. "Look, I gotta get back. You do those exercises, and hang in there. I'll see you at the fair, okay?"

"Thanks, Luke," I said, and blew out a sigh, relieved to have this mortifying conversation behind me. So much for retaining shreds of my dignity, huh?

Slipping out the door, I was suddenly grateful for the familiar sight of my old ten-speed. I rolled my neck to try to release some of the tension, then strapped my helmet back on. I was eager to pedal away, to try to feel normal again. Whatever normal was.

But what was most important, I told myself, was that

I was no longer taking Heartless's heartlessness lying down. I had a real and viable plan in place now to turn things around.

And in the meantime, I had twelve days until the sports fair. Studying up on kissing had to be easier than geometry and biology, right? And a lot more fun. Besides, the bottom line was that this had far greater consequences than just getting a decent report card.

I had to keep my name from turning from Parker Elizabeth Stanhope into . . . well, Mud.

Butterfly Kisses:
When two people put their open eyes close together and flutter their eyelashes.

Since I was in the neighborhood, I made a pit stop at my brother's dorm. I found him on the side patio, slapping a coat of paint on a chest of drawers I recognized from our attic. I knew he'd said he wanted his dorm room to have a cleaner look this year, but I had thought he'd simply meant getting the pizza boxes and dirty clothes off the carpet. Good to see him really stepping up.

"Luke's in," I told him, balancing the bike and myself on the pavement.

With golden curls he hadn't cut in ages and bushy blond eyebrows, Clayton had started to look like the

Cowardly Lion from *The Wizard of Oz*. Especially when he smiled and his cheeks puffed up, like now. "I knew we could count on him."

"But he says I have to work on my kissing skills, that I have to make it look real."

He paused mid-brushstroke and glanced up at me. "He's probably right. But just an FYI? Brothers don't generally like to talk about their sisters kissing people. Even when it's business rather than pleasure."

"Oh, are you suggesting I take this little problem to Dad?" I asked in mock innocence.

Paintbrush firmly between two fingers, Clayton flung his arms up over his head as if a bomb were about to fall from the sky. I couldn't help but laugh at his expression.

"God, no!" he yelled, then chuckled and dropped his arms. "I'll let you take care of that kissing stuff, Parker, while I keep my mind on the legal angle and how we're going to hang your coach with her own words."

"Sounds fair." I grinned and hopped back on my bike.

What was that saying about all being fair in love and war? Well, this qualified as war.

Minutes later, I was in a nearby supermarket check-out line, my head down, mentally willing the lady ahead of me to hurry. I'd been embarrassed buying feminine-hygiene products in the past, but that was nothing compared with buying an economy-sized bag of Starbursts and a basket of bing cherries. If Luke's ex knew they were good kissing-improvement devices, others had to, too, right? I mean, come on, who buys bing cherries?

I half expected some idiot to notice and toss me a tube of Chap Stick or the address of a support group for bad kissers. What I didn't expect was to recognize the cashier. With her trademark thatch of dark hair and the Madonna-like beauty mark on her cheek, my middle school best friend and current *ex*—best friend, Becca Benvenuto, was unmistakable.

We'd met the week before seventh grade, grabbing the same size-four extralong jeans in Anna Banana's Boutique in Old Town. Then, recognizing each other in class, we'd started talking and became friends—soon, best friends. And by eighth grade, we had this thing going where we'd simply sign notes "Your BFF."

But high school has a way of steering people in different directions, and while I'd fallen in with the soccer girls, she'd gone . . . well, somewhere else. I mean, whenever I saw her in the halls or cafeteria, she was with people.

"Hey, Becca," I said, smiling big to will her attention to my face and away from my odd purchases.

"Parker." She nodded, reaching for my family-sized candy bag. "What are you doing all the way over here?"

My brain reeled. I didn't want any "proof" of my planning meeting with Luke. "Visiting Clayton at school," I said, only half lying.

"What's he now, a junior?"

"Sophomore."

But instead of keeping up her end of the conversation, she just grunted and read me the total. Fine by me. I sooo wanted this over. "Okay, then," I said, a little loud, as I paid. "Uh, have a nice end of summer. See you at school next week, huh?"

Becca looked at me, straining, as if a reply was circling in her head but couldn't find its way out. I was so sure she was seeing through my purchases. And how embarrassing would that be? Then all she did was say "Uh-huh," hand me my sack, and turn to her next customer.

As I left, I told myself I was paranoid. It made sense that a stud like Luke and the girls he'd go for would be wise to things guy-girl intimate. But that didn't necessarily hold for the average person. Like, look at Chrissandra, who was totally popular. And . . . Mandy and Elaine and me. We held our own in the status-sphere, but even in all our sleepover chats, we'd never talked about cherries and Starbursts.

My secret was still safe.

Traffic was backed up along the cobblestone-edged streets of Old Town, so I cut over to the industrial district. Aside from getting my fair share of exhaust fumes and hey-baby toots from truck drivers—I'd learned a long time ago that lecherous guys go for tall blondes—I made good time, even crossing the Aerial Lift Bridge to our Lake Superior island without having to wait for the bridge's midsection to rise to let a trawler or high-mast sailboat through.

I decided these were good signs, proof that everything was moving with me now rather than against me. And surely our neighbors' gardeners, whose wooden-slatted truck had spit out freshly mowed grass onto the street that morning, had come back to clean up. I'd chased the truck down on my bike, soaring through two stop signs to make up for the fact that my wheels only went a fraction as fast as theirs.

They'd pulled their rickety truck over and listened while I'd huffed out my request. I knew I'd come off like a crazed neat freak, but the gardeners didn't work for my dad or Mr. Murphy, across the street, and didn't have a *clue* the can of worms they'd be opening if they left that mess in the street between our houses.

Rounding the corner of my street, I kept my gaze low, looking for residual blades of bright green. But my attention was quickly stolen by the tall, broad figure in the center of the street, pushing a broom. I realized with a sinking feeling that the gardeners had laughed at the silly girl on the old bike and driven off.

And that my across-the-street neighbor, Tristan Murphy, was taking matters into his own hands (literally) to help keep the peace.

I had to thank him. Which was even further out of my comfort zone than buying learn-to-kiss items. I mean, aside from the proximity of our houses and the fact that our fathers were embroiled in a ridiculous, unreasonable and thoroughly embarrassing feud, Tristan and I had nothing in common. We passed silently, like ships in the night, sometimes while he was shooting baskets in his driveway, sometimes waiting for the bridge to rise, sometimes in town. And breaking that silence would be awkward, to say the least.

I was two grades ahead of him in school, although he'd told me at a neighborhood barbecue when he and his dad had first moved to DeGroot that he'd started school late because of a fall birthday. I had a fall birthday, too, and over Orange Crushes, guacamole and chips, we'd calculated that he was only 364 days younger than me.

But whatever. For the past couple of years, he'd been at the middle school. And now it was almost worse. He was a freshman at DHS. And *freshman* was a very dirty word to me right now. It went arm in arm with *JV* and "friends nervously avoiding me." I didn't want to admit freshmen existed, let alone speak to one. God, I felt like a loser.

Reasonably, I did know it wasn't his fault that Heartless had lost her mind. And he *was* out here doing reconnaissance to prevent World War III from breaking out on Millard Circle, so breaking our silence was the least I could do.

"Hey," I said, my brakes squeaking to a curbside stop.

He glanced over, his head much higher above mine than last time I'd looked. He'd somehow shot up to about six feet and had maybe started weight lifting, because he suddenly had more upper body than ever before, too.

He may have only been fifteen, but I figured he could get into R-rated movies, no problem. Still, he had the *F* for *freshman* seared into his forehead, so I had to make this quick.

"I talked to the gardeners who did this," I said, pointing to the grass that was now squashed down flat, thanks to the numerous sets of tires that had ridden over it. "They promised to come back and clean it up. But clearly, they lied."

"You think?" he said, a tinge of good-natured humor touching his sarcasm.

I took off my helmet and gave my head a shake, but I didn't need a mirror to know my hair was most likely sweaty and hanging limp down my back. Like I said, "carelessly tousled" would be a compliment.

"Some of this stuff just won't sweep up," he said. "I think we're going to need a spade to scrape it."

I hooked my helmet around my handlebars. "We probably have one. I think my dad's got every tool and gadget ever *invented* now, to make sure our house is in tip-top shape."

"Tell me about it," he said, with a grimace that suggested he was every bit as embarrassed by his dad's juvenile behavior as I was by my dad's. "Since this thing between them began, we've become like a mini version of Home Depot." He nodded toward his open garage. "There's a spade hanging on the wall above the workbench. Can you go grab it? I mean, if you're not afraid to enter enemy territory."

I did an exaggerated "Ooh, ooh," like, *Oh, yeah, I'm so scared;* then I leaned my bike against the curb. My helmet and plastic grocery sack came to hard rests on the pavement, and a bright red edge of the family-sized bag of Starburst slid out.

"Hey, Starburst," he said.

"Help yourself."

"Yeah?"

"Go crazy." Turning toward the garage, I heard a car cruise past. I hoped it didn't squish more grass. "Over the workbench, you said?" I called back.

"You can't miss it."

I made my way to the garage, knowing what I *could* miss was our dads coming home to this mess. Each would blame the other, resulting in heated conversations with anyone who'd listen, including city officials.

This all dated back about a year, when "someone" (and don't get my dad started on how he knew it was Mr. Murphy) called the city zoning office about the height of our cinder-block wall. It turned out we were eleven inches over code, and we'd had to remove one block all around the wall.

My father had been furious, and since then, when he wasn't doing outdoor improvements, he was standing like a sea captain at the highest point of our front yard, his hand blocking the sun, surveying every visible inch of the Murphys' property for code infractions. Or calling Clayton, asking him to check the university's law texts for special variances and loopholes.

All I could say was thank God our street dead-ended, which kept traffic to a minimum, so only the neighbors saw his insanity, not all of DeGroot.

Mr. Murphy, who hotly denied being the whistle-blower, was quick to bad-eye my dad right back and now claimed to have the zoning office on speed dial to report us for any violations.

Never had two yards been tidier, better landscaped, or two houses more freshly painted. It had long gone from get-a-life Dad to get-a-grip Dad, but I realize now that there's just some crap in your life you have to roll your eyes at and accept.

Not including my JV status.

I found the spade easily and headed back outside.

Tristan was ripping open the bag of candy with his teeth. "I've been meaning to talk to you about the gutter on the north side of your house," he said when I got within earshot. "Some of the paint is chipping."

I arched a brow.

"Someone could report you."

"Someone," I said flatly.

"Just saying."

"No one that you know? That you're related to or are descended from?"

He grabbed a Starburst square, then handed me the bag. I set it on the curb.

"And if we fix it?" I went on, squatting down to scrape at a stubborn patch of smashed grass. "If we re-paint? You won't call the city?"

"Not me. But I'm cool like that."

I wasn't sure if he was playing with me or giving me a legitimate warning, but I knew I'd be checking out the gutter when I got home. In any case, I had to give him some credit for humor and any steps he was taking to keep our dads' turf war from escalating. I glanced up to give him a full-on smile.

Only to see him pulling a Starburst wrapper off his tongue.

Chills: Don't be afraid to experiment. Chills will rush down his spine when you gently lick his lips.

"How . . . where did you learn to do that?" I tried to keep the surprise out of my voice but had no idea if I was actually successful.

He dropped the wet wrapper into the green waste. "Camp." He stared at me like I should know what that meant. "I was gone most of the summer, Parker. I was a counselor at Etiwanda."

"Oh," I said, and nodded like I'd noticed he'd been gone. Maybe that explained how I'd missed his growth spurt? "Sure."

"Not much to do there after lights-out. So the

counselors got together in our cabins for some fun and games. You know?"

"What do you mean, *kissing* games?" I asked, sort of shocked at myself for getting so personal, and horrified at the prospect of what he might say.

He screwed up his face into a look that read: *Uh . . . yeah.* "Seven minutes in heaven, spin the bottle, truth or dare. And some I'm not even sure had names." He studied my face. "Why? You think that's stupid?"

"No!" He gave me a "What's your problem?" look, so I took a breath and continued. "No," I said again, calmer. "I don't suppose you know how to make a loop with a cherry stem, too?"

"Why?"

"Just asking."

He pointed at my supermarket bag. "You got cherries in there?"

I nodded.

"I set the record. A loop in forty-eight seconds."

Jeez, what kind of camp did he work at? And was it too late to sign up?

He leaned against the broom handle. "What's with the sudden interest in camp? Or, should I say kissing? Is your boyfriend complaining?"

I choked out a laugh. "No. No complaints." From any guys. Yet. "Just—well, I mean, who couldn't stand to get a little better?"

He held my gaze long enough for me to realize that his eyes were dark blue—like the deepest part of a lake or the sapphire birthstone I was hoping to get set in my senior-class ring. But I couldn't decide if that color looked good in a person's *face* or not. . . .

"You want me to show you my cherry looping?"

I considered it. Then I realized I wouldn't be able to see anything but the end result. So I shook my head, then shrugged as if this had been a silly conversation anyway and went back to my scraping.

He clearly got the message that we'd moved on, because he laid down his broom and set off toward his garage. Moments later, his return was announced by the rolling of trash-can wheels. Stopping in the street, he scooped a clump of grass into a dust pan, chucked it in the trash, then turned to me.

"So who is he?"

"Huh?"

"The new guy. When I left for camp, you and your boyfriend had broken up. Or so people were saying. Who's this one? A senior?"

I just stared at him.

First of all, incoming freshmen were talking about my love life? Really? I mean, I knew playing soccer gave me a certain visibility, and being friends with Chrissandra Hickey was only good for anyone's rep. But the idea that stats on my life had trickled down to the middle school level astonished me.

And then there was the problem of how to respond. There *was* no new guy. Luke didn't count. He was just . . . Luke. And no way was I explaining about Heartless and varsity. "I can't really talk about it," I finally said, and did a Chrissandra-like hair toss that I hoped would shut him up.

"What, it's in the works?"

I frowned.

"You're trying to steal a guy away from someone?"

Wait a minute—I didn't want *that* kind of gossip going around about me. But would it really be worse than the plain truth? I just shrugged. Not a yes, not a no.

"You can probably pull it off."

I didn't know how to respond to that, so I was just as happy that he kept talking.

"If you're looking to make real points with the guy, I can fill you in on some things. You know, like different techniques—Caterpillar Kisses, Butterfly Kisses. And the Steam Kiss—"

"Whoa," I said, putting my hand up. It was starting to feel like he was the one about to be a junior all of a sudden, and I was the know-nothing ninth grader. Even if I *did* know nothing about these things.

"Oh, do you know all this stuff?" he asked, his gaze challenging mine as he rested his broom against the trash can.

"Sure." I stood up to look him in the eye. I might have been a few inches shorter, but I'd had two years of drills from Heartless on how to stare down your opponent.

"Yeah, so what's a Steam Kiss?"

A no-brainer (probably). "A kiss that's so hot that

imaginary steam comes out of your partner's ears." Did I just say that?

He made an irritating sound like a game-show buzzer. "Wrong. What's a Caterpillar Kiss?"

I had to admit my confidence was slipping. All I could think was, two people lying stomach-down on the ground with their heads up so their mouths could meet.

Tristan must have seen the confusion in my eyes, because the next thing I knew, he was in my face.

"Tell you what, Parker. I'll show you."

"Show me?" I wasn't at all sure I liked where this was going.

"Don't worry, our lips won't even touch. Just stay where you are, and don't move."

I wanted to move, all right, to thrust my palms forward to keep this neighbor-boy froshie *out* of my body space. Who did he think he was?

But I was also hungry for knowledge. So I did a quick scan to make sure the street was empty and there would be no witnesses. And I told myself that as long as our lips stayed apart, it wouldn't count as an official kiss, which could come back to haunt me. Right?

I locked my limbs in cautious anticipation and looked up at Tristan Murphy's dark blue eyes as he stepped in closer. And closer.

He must have bent his knees, because his eyes suddenly were level with mine. Then his hands secured themselves on my upper arms, and he leaned in until his eyebrows were pushed up against mine. I thought I

23

might laugh—not that anything was funny—but steeled myself into paying attention in case I decided to use this on Luke.

Tristan tilted his head so that our foreheads touched, then started this gentle crisscross motion, rubbing our eyebrows. It kind of tickled, and made me want to laugh, or at least smile—if not at the sensation, then at what we were doing.

But it also felt good—silky and soft. Making me forget the silliness, making me want to get closer, to snuggle up—

Wait. What was I thinking?

I should be pushing him back onto his property. Because—gah!—what was I doing in a face smush with the Murphy kid?

He must have sensed my change of heart, because he pulled back. Or maybe he was just finished.

"That," he said, like some sort of campus professor on the subject, "was a Caterpillar Kiss. It's all about the eyebrows. And a Butterfly Kiss starts out the same, but it's the bringing together of eyelashes."

"I'll take your word for it," I said, shuffling on the pavement to regain my full balance. And to take back the power.

"And the Steam Kiss—"

"Enough," I said sharply.

"Okay, well, we couldn't do that one outside, anyway."

Something strangled in my throat. *What?* Like we'd

only do it behind closed doors? Omigod, this was moving into out-of-hand territory. I shook my head and composed myself. "Look, you can finish up here without me, right?"

He shrugged.

"Because I gotta go." I was suddenly incredibly uncomfortable.

"Okay," he answered, as if he knew something I didn't. "But if there's anything I can do to help you with this guy, just ask. You know, I can be discreet."

"Don't tell me," I said flatly, "—you're cool like that?"

A frown settled slowly into his brow, and for a long moment, he just stared at me. "What, you're mad now? You're the one who brought the cherries and the Starburst over. You're the one who wanted to know about camp and kissing games."

Crap—he was right. "Yeah, well," I said, pulling my bike off the curb, "I guess I thought it was sort of cute. You know, how freshmen fill their time while waiting for their lives to begin." I didn't intend to be mean; it just sort of spilled out of my mouth.

I could see anger spark in his eyes. "Like *you* can talk. Sixteen and never been kissed."

"I've been kissed!" Suddenly I was okay with mean. I found my balance and set off on my bike, not even bothering with my helmet.

"The back of your hand does not count!"

I circled back around, not entirely sure what I was going to say, hoping it would somehow be brilliant.

But his voice cut through the air. "You'd better find someone to teach you this stuff, Parker, if you're ever going to *keep* a boyfriend. Because it sure won't be with your sparkling personality!"

I pedaled fast in a full circle, pretending not to hear. Little did Tristan know that keeping a boyfriend was the least of my worries. All I was concerned with was keeping my friends and my place on the team alongside them.

As well as keeping my cool. And the last thing I needed was my *own* neighbor feud.

Diversify: Vary the tempo, intensity and duration of kisses to keep things interesting.

I parked my bike in the garage, then circled around to the side of the house to check the gutters. Cupping my hand against the sun, I saw that they were perfectly, flawlessly, don't-mess-with-me painted.

Looked like the frosh had just been messing with me. As if I needed more drama in my life.

Upstairs in my room, I flopped onto my bed and considered quitting high school. Going for an equivalency diploma would certainly save me from taking this whole Heartless heartache to heart, and from having to learn about kissing. Plus, it would make things right with my friends. I mean, if I wasn't at school, why would they have to worry about watching their mouths to protect my feelings?

Yeah, it was the answer. If you didn't take into account that (1) my parents would go postal, (2) a GED wasn't exactly the fast track to the kind of university I was targeting, and (3) it was pointless to get my friends back if I wasn't at school to hang out with them.

After a long sigh, I dragged myself over to my computer to see what the word *kiss* brought up in a search engine. I mean, was there a book called *Kissing for Dummies* or something?

I signed on to IM and saw a few people on, including Chrissandra.

Before I got the chance to double-click on her name, the house phone rang. I felt my breath catch as I rushed to grab the old-fashioned princess extension in my parents' bedroom, hoping desperately it was for me.

"Hello?" I said, willing Chrissandra's voice to respond.

"Parker," she said. "I saw you come online."

I didn't know whether to laugh or cry. Hearing her voice again was *just so great*. Cheddar-cheese-popcorn-and-Drew-Barrymore-movies-at-two-a.m.-in-our-sleeping-bags great.

"Hey!" I said, practically yelling, I was so happy. But that was okay, because this was Chrissandra, and clearly things were getting back to normal.

"You have to promise not to tell anyone I called," she said, her voice dropping.

What? No *Hey, how have you been, my best friend Parker?* I felt myself slowly going numb, from the inside out. "Okay. Why?"

"I'm not supposed to tell you—it kind of defeats the purpose. But when you see us from now on—Mandy, Elaine and me—we're not going to welcome you with open arms or anything. That's why I'm calling—we've decided to cut you loose."

If complete and utter horror made a sound, I swear, I made it.

"It's because we love you, Parker," she added quickly. "Since you're on JV again, you need to be free to hang out with your new teammates."

Oh, God.

The thing was, despite the fact that Chrissandra came off as a queen bee, those who buzzed around liked to think it was pretty much an act. That deep down, she was thoughtful and caring, and she wouldn't do anything she didn't honestly think was right. At least, anything that had to do with us.

"No, Chrissandra," I said, wrapping the phone cord around a finger and hearing the pleading in my voice, "I am *not* one of them. I don't belong on JV. It's only be-cause that awful Rachael came back and that other girl transferred in from out of state."

"We know that. But solidarity is the key to winning, after all, so you have to stay with your team. Just like we have to stay with ours."

With fear constricting my throat, I did not respond.

"We know we're going to come off like total bitches

to everyone else, but we need you to know the truth. That it's not personal, okay? And we really hope you make varsity soon and can come back to us."

My brain reeling, I spoke with as much dignity as possible.

"Well, what if I quit soccer? Altogether?"

She was silent for a long moment, then finally said, "Don't you think that's overkill?"

Wait—like *I* was the drama queen? With her theatrical temperament, she had commanded JV soccer, as well as the freshman/sophomore corridors. As her grateful hangers-on, whatever Chrissandra did, Mandy, Elaine and I did. Whatever she wore, we wore. Whatever she thought was cool, we thought was cool. We even dug deep for authentic-sounding enthusiasm for yet another viewing of Leonardo DiCaprio and Claire Danes as Romeo and Juliet, when what we really wanted to see again was *Bend It Like Beckham*.

Guys flocked around her, too. And last winter, when she decided she wanted catalog model Kyle Fenske, she went after him with the intensity of a white-hot sun. And he gave in without much of a fight. There had been some hallway jokes about how much prettier Kyle was than Chrissandra, including ones calling their relationship "interfacial." But Kyle seemed as devoted to her as she was to him, and I had to admit, she'd been easier to get along with since she'd hooked up with him.

Until all this, of course.

"But if I weren't on a soccer team at all . . . ," I tried

again, then sank down onto the carpet between my parents' twin beds, holding on to the phone for dear life. My neck was tensing up, the sweat was back in my hairline, and I wasn't entirely sure the Starbursts I'd popped were going to stay down.

"Look, Park, it's only four days till school starts. I'm sure you'll work it out with Coach and everything will be okay."

"Chrissandra . . ."

"It has to be this way. You know that." She seemed to sigh. "See you at school. And make sure you look fab-u, okay? And act like you're totally in control. Do not show fear."

"Yeah," I simply said, knowing pure terror would prevent me from having any other emotions.

I spent the next couple of hours on the Internet, trying to absorb all I could about kissing. I told myself that Luke and I would impress the school with a kiss as beautiful as the one the couple shared in *The Princess Bride,* "the most passionate, the most pure" kiss of all time.

My vision was, of course, a gross exaggeration, since Westley and Buttercup were madly in love, and I was just madly committed to fooling Heartless. Still, it was something to aim for—and far better than worrying about a situation I could do very little about.

Knowing that Chrissandra would turn pea green with envy when I lip-smacked with Luke didn't hurt, either. Like so many others, she had it bad for him, and it amazed her that I didn't. I couldn't count how many times she'd asked if I'd accidentally-on-purpose seen parts of Luke I shouldn't have when he'd slept at our house, or if I'd ever overheard what really and truly turned him on in a girl.

Like I'd repeat those things if I had.

But now that she held my fate in her hands, I wished I did have dirt to dish. Anything to make her get behind me again. Because, as part of Chrissandra's inner circle, you were rewarded with unconditional protection from the cruel, cruel world. Sort of like being a goon for Tony Soprano, only with fewer *F* words and no guns. But like with Tony, when Chrissandra turned her back on you, you knew you'd better run.

A voice from my past blew like a hurricane through my thoughts. Something about *What goes around comes around,* but it was gone almost as fast as it had arrived, leaving me with sort of a bad taste in my mouth that might as easily have been from all the Starbursts I'd eaten. It seemed like a good time to put it all aside for a bit and wander downstairs toward the kitchen noise. Maybe dinner would help me feel a little better.

My mother, Joan Stanhope, stood before the open refrigerator in her stocking feet, the sleeves of her white blouse rolled back. She's one of the few grown-ups I've known who truly love their work—she teaches kindergarteners. And even though this week she was only doing classroom setup, it was still her style to give it her all and come home exhausted.

"What's the verdict on dinner?" I asked, and moved

in for a fast hug, which included a welcome blast of re-frigerated air.

My mother smiled. It was a pretty smile—white and wide. People said I had it, too, but I couldn't see it. "Omelets?"

"Yeah, but isn't Dad weird about having 'breakfast for dinner'?"

"It's either that," she said wearily, "or I go to the store."

"Well, we could tell him that someone from the city was out to inspect the Murphys' yard. He'll be so over-joyed, he won't notice what he's eating."

She shot me a look. Ever since my father got pro-moted to regional manager at his insurance office, she'd instigated this strict "Do not stress out your father; he gets enough of that at work" rule. I'd noticed that lately it had been extended to not joking about him or talking bad about him behind his back, too, as if somehow those negative vibes would find their way to his psyche through the cosmos.

"Just saying," I said, and shrugged.

She moved the egg carton to the counter and changed the subject to ask about my day. I thought about telling her about the gardeners' truck, but that circled my thoughts back to the eyebrow kiss and neighbor boy's strange offer to teach me about kissing. Something I did not want to dwell on.

Instead, I talked about my idea for a first-day-of-school outfit (one that I was sure Chrissandra and the girls would love).

"Anna Banana's has this fab-u skirt in the window," I said, using Chrissandra's favorite word. "Gray, with these ballerina-like frills peeking out of the bottom. With a tank top, and maybe a black cardigan and my rhinestone ballet flats, it could be really cute."

"Uh-huh. But how are you going to be paying for that?"

I did the *duh* look. She'd pay—like always. My parents were pretty generous when it came to my clothing allowance. But instead of grinning, she gave me a serious look, changing my *duh* to *huh?*

"Where are you standing with soccer right now?" she asked, which seemed like a radical change of subjects but which my heart of hearts told me was tragically related. "Are you still planning to show up for that first JV practice?"

"Yeah," I said carefully.

"Okay, then. You can use my debit card. But Parker, we've talked about this. Your father and I want you to keep playing, even if it's on JV. Exercise, teamwork and staying busy are important components of high school success."

Yeah, yeah. I'd heard this several times the past couple of weeks. And filed it away with their other pre-packaged lectures about always doing one's best, reaching for the stars, saving oneself for marriage, etc. But this was the first time I'd heard an "or else" attached.

"So you're saying," I said, and let out a laugh at the unfairness and sheer irony, "if I quit JV, no more new outfits?"

34

"I'm reminding you that your father and I have certain standards for you and your brother, and the 'extras' only come after you've met them. Cute outfits are extra."

I felt my jaw drop to my feet. If I stayed on JV to please my parents, I could have a great wardrobe—and no friends. If I quit to try to get my friends back, I'd have to wear last year's rags, which would *so* not fly with Chrissandra. She'd give me the boot anyway.

The muscles in my shoulders and neck felt like they were creeping together to form one long, angry knot. And a wave of anger and panic and probably some other emotions I was too upset to identify swept me toward the back door. I grabbed the handle.

"Dinner's going to be ready in fifteen minutes."

Like I could think about eating.

"Parker, where are you going?"

"Out," I said, and slammed the door behind me.

Somewhere. Anywhere.

I stomped across the side lawn, the pressure of my footsteps reverberating in my head. I looked to see the white two-story house across the street, all pristine and perfect, thanks to my father's revenge obsession.

Cringing at what I suddenly knew I needed to do, I crossed the asphalt to go knock on the door. I needed to apologize for the rude way I'd left things before and see if Tristan was still game for helping me.

Because right now, Tristan Murphy seemed like my best shot at saving what remained of my life.

Eyes: Closed is the preference of sixty-six percent of kissers.

As if things weren't weird enough, Mr. Murphy answered the door. He was tall, like Tristan, but with less hair and more nose. And, incidentally, without the red horns that Dad seemed to think he hid under his Twins baseball hat. After a cursory glance at me, Mr. Murphy arched a brow.

"Tell your father I've got the sprinkler heads on order and that County Ordinance Six Sixteen states I have thirty days to comply."

"Uh . . . I don't know anything about that. I'm here to speak to Tristan."

"Tristan?" He shifted his weight. "You know Tristan?"

I guess he didn't remember that long-ago summer barbecue. I nodded. If I got my way, I was about to know his son a whole lot better.

Mr. Murphy backed away, and in as little time as it took to clear my throat, Tristan filled the doorway. He wore a gray T-shirt that said "DeGroot High School Water Polo" and a curious expression. Fleetingly, I wondered what he'd had on earlier and realized that all I could remember was how nicely he had filled out. I'd mostly been looking away—or close up, into his eyes. Could this day *get* any more bizarre?

"Parker," he said, sounding remotely amused.

"Yeah. Uh, you up for a walk?"

He nodded as if it was the most normal thing he'd ever been asked and followed me outside. In unspoken agreement, we headed toward the street corner, which led out to the harbor.

"So how come you're not riding that high-tech bike tonight?"

I shot him a look. I knew I deserved at least one jab for my behavior earlier, but if Tristan and I were going to work together—especially with him in the leadership role—I was going to have to keep a strong upper hand.

"I thought I'd rely on my own two legs this time," I told him, then offered up a sweet smile. I'd seen Chrissandra wrap guys around her little finger a million times, so, while bald-faced manipulation didn't come

37

naturally to me, I had studied at the feet of the master. "And my big mouth—to say sorry about before. I know I kind of went off on you."

He lifted his eyebrows. "Kind of."

"I'm under a lot of pressure right now."

"Uh-huh, I know—trying to get your hands on that new guy."

Wow, he wasn't going to make this easy. But I no longer had time for games. This was about life and death. At least of my social life.

"Look, I came to apologize. *And* to ask for your help. When Luke Anderson buys a kiss from me at the sports-fair kissing booth, I need to make sure he publicly gets his money's worth."

"Huh?" He stopped midstride. "Luke Anderson? Oh, the prom king. The college guy. I see. . . . So you're playing in a whole new league."

"It's actually way more complicated than that."

He fell back into step with me, and we crossed the grassy knoll that overlooked the harbor. An older couple sat on a bench, looking out at the choppy waters, while a little kid from the end of our street walked his dog.

"It all comes down to the fact," I said, and took a deep breath—it would never be easy to say—"that I didn't make varsity soccer."

Even though he looked confused as to what varsity had to do with kissing a prom king (as well he should have), his tone softened. "That's gotta suck."

"Yeah, and since there's a player limit, Coach says

my best bet's to sit tight on JV and wait to see if there's an opening."

"Wow, a junior on JV. That's got to be about as embarrassing as kissing your sister."

I laughed; I couldn't help it. He pretty much hit that on the nose. Then I regrouped. "Sadly, I just found out that my parents are all for that, too. And my friends aren't helping any. They're basically ignoring me until I get moved up."

He made a sympathetic noise.

"The only other person who has done anything to help is my brother. He's come up with a crazy-but-just-might-work plan and talked Luke into jumping on board."

Wind whipped off the water, tousling Tristan's hair and blowing mine around my head like a turban. I pushed some strands away and saw the baffled look on his face.

"So, what?" he asked, his brow wrinkled. "I'm not really getting the connection here."

"It's more straightforward than you'd think," I said. And then, as we strolled the walkway along the harbor's edge—under the bridge, across the jetty, toward the lighthouse—I spelled out the specifics.

"Actually," I concluded, pausing against the concrete along the wall of the jetty, "I think it might work. It's a little crappy, since it *does* involve someone getting bumped off the team, but I'm hoping Hartley will take care of that herself."

Tristan did a "not bad, not bad" purse of his mouth, adding that he'd heard how important prime parking spaces were at DeGroot High School.

"But what I don't get," he said, his back pressed against the wall and his eyes on me, "is where I come in. How can I help you?"

My lungs suddenly felt tight. I didn't want to have to say it out loud, but no one had ever said this would be pretty. "I want you to show me what you learned in camp. Like before. Only . . . you know, everything, so I can choose what will work best with Luke."

I thought he might laugh or maybe even make a lips-first lunge at me. I mean, freshmen aren't exactly known for their maturity and patience, right? What I did not anticipate was a creased brow, followed by a slow shake of his head.

"You mean your ex didn't show you all you need to know?"

Ugh—that again. I think Tristan thought more about my ex than I did, and he'd never even met the guy. "He lived an hour away."

"Still . . ."

I shook my head. "Even when we were together, we didn't have much, you know, alone time."

"The guy didn't make it his mission to find times and places to be with you? Good thing you dumped his ass."

The breakup was mutual—something had just flickered and died out—but it didn't serve my purposes to go into the details. Tristan needed to think of me as a take-charge person.

"Look," I said instead, "this arrangement has to be a total secret. If anyone finds out about these 'lessons,' the whole thing blows up in my face. Like, nuclear, don't-even-*bother*-trying-to-get-my-friends-back big."

He shrugged, like, *Well, duh.*

"And remember," I went on, "this is work. And nothing to do with fun or taking things any further."

"Work," he repeated, looking out at the water. "So what's in it for me?"

I felt my jaw drop. What—making out with a popular (or at least formerly popular) junior wasn't "payment" enough? Thankfully, I managed a more politically correct response. "Well, since Luke's got all my money, I'm broke. But I suppose I could pay you a hundred bucks. In installments," I added.

"I don't want your money, Parker." The light in his dark eyes seemed to flicker, then return in full wattage. "I'll tell you what I do want."

I bit back a smile. Oh, I knew what he wanted, too, and I had to give him credit for dreaming so big! But the good news was that his alleged desire for my bod shifted the power right back to me. Where I wanted it. Where it belonged. (Chrissandra would be proud of me.) So I smiled and I wagged a finger. "Careful, Sparky. Don't say anything you're going to regret and ruin this thing before it even starts."

"What I want is for you to acknowledge me in school."

I studied his face. *Huh?*

"Say hello when we pass in the hall. Pause when I'm

talking to a bunch of guys, and ask or tell me something. Show people I am worth knowing."

Wow. My head was spinning. This guy was unpredictable.

And I was flattered. Except that being seen talking to him in public felt dangerous. Like ditching school or writing test notes under your sleeve. It would be flaunting convention, practically daring people to figure out what was going on with us. And that wasn't my style. I was a by-the-book girl, a team player—

Except look where that had gotten me.

"Okay," I said, a little uncertainly. I really didn't have much to lose at this point. "Sure."

"Good." He smiled. "Then I'll do it."

"Do what?"

"Go along with your plan."

My words escaped before I had a chance to catch them. "You mean . . . you weren't going to?"

Tristan laughed. *He laughed?*

Then he flicked his head back toward land. "Come on. I've got to get home for dinner."

Dinner. Oh, yeah. My omelet was probably as cold and flat as those blades of grass we'd scraped up earlier.

"When do we want to start?" he continued.

My brain raced. "How about after my parents leave for work tomorrow? Just come over."

He nodded.

We fell into step together, his legs longer than mine but the two of us somehow creating a balanced rhythm.

And while a voice in the back of my head warned that Tristan might not be easy to handle, for the first time all day, my muscles weren't tense, and I suspected I'd soon be able to have whole thoughts on topics that did not include my sucky life.

Passing under the bridge, I glanced Tristan's way. It wasn't until I saw the smile start to pull at his mouth that I realized I was smiling, too.

Focus: When French-kissing, focus on keeping your tongues inside each other's mouths. Otherwise, it's more like puppy-dog-licking.

My mother was sitting at the kitchen table when I got home, tapping an impatient foot. Her and Dad's dirty dishes had been cleared to the counter, telling me I was later than late. My dad was nowhere to be seen, but the steady pounding out back was a big clue that he was around and working on yet another home-improvement project.

I managed an apology; then I told her why I'd stormed off. "I just feel like everything's coming down on me at once," I went on, hoping to shift the mood to one that included sympathy.

"I'm on your side, Parker. I really am. But I've heard of too many teens wasting their lives in front of screens. It's important to me that you stay fit and active."

In this case, staying fit and active also meant staying stressed. But I could see we were mending fences, so I simply shrugged.

"Where were you all this time?"

"Out walking." In case anyone had seen me with Tristan and reported it back to her, I added, "With the Murphy kid. He's starting DHS this year, and I, uh, offered to help him settle in." (Conveniently leaving out all he was doing for me.)

"You two are becoming friendly?"

I shrugged one shoulder.

"Actually, that might be a good idea. I think half the reason your father keeps up this ridiculous property battle is ignorance. For some reason, he's got it in his head that George Murphy is evil. Maybe you can invite this Tristan over, and your dad can see for himself that the kid is not the spawn of the devil and start to humanize the situation."

"Maybe," I said, thinking of the strange make-out session Tristan and I had planned for the living room sofa as soon as my parents left for work in the morning. If my dad walked in on *that*, things would escalate from bad blood to Armageddon.

My mother patted my arm, then warmed my omelet, which I accepted with equal parts appreciation and guilt.

I'd only taken a few bites when my father cruised

through the back door. He was dressed in a varnish-stained T-shirt, saggy jeans and cracked work boots—his standard around the house after he shed his brand-name suits.

"Hey, Dad," I said, and braced myself for the where-have-you-been-young-lady routine.

But he just patted my head. "And here I thought you'd gotten a better offer for dinner."

Sensing the chance to lighten things up, I grinned. "You mean like Prince Harry cruised into the harbor on his royal British yacht and offered me lobster?"

His eyes twinkled. "That, or anything that constituted a *real* dinner."

I threw a look at Mom. "See? What did I tell you? I knew eggs wouldn't fly."

Mom sighed. "Oh, the things I put you two through."

I could have snorted and agreed—but it was kind of nice to have peace back in the house, so I simply went back to eating.

The next morning, I busied myself picking up the living room. I wasn't nervous, exactly (okay, maybe a little), but it *was* pretty weird to imagine locking lips with a guy I'd lived by for years and yet barely knew. Weirder still that it was going to happen *in my house,* and in the morning. At least if we were at a party, with music and friends and little or no lighting to take the edge off . . .

As I moved some magazines to my room, my eyes fell upon a seal-colored Furby doll that had been batteryless and "sleeping" on my shelf for years. Mom had tried to give it away or throw it out several times, but I'd dug in my heels, the memory of how desperately I'd wanted it, and how hard I'd worked for it with household chores and a lemonade stand, keeping its value high. Making it impossible to part with. I'd even taken good care of it long after its novelty had worn off.

I heard a door slam across the street, and images of the Furby and Tristan knocked together in my head. Idly, I hoped the Plan wouldn't be a repeat of my Furby incident, where getting what I wanted hadn't lived up to the goal and the chase.

The knock on the door was the equivalent of the first bell at school. Class was about to begin. I was suddenly as anxious about letting Tristan in as I expected to feel when I took that long, lonely walk down the hallway on Monday without Chrissandra or Mandy or any of my other friends. But I knew if I wanted my life back, there was a price to pay. And it started with putting my mouth where my money was. So I opened the door.

"Hey," Tristan said. "Coast clear?"

"Yeah."

His hair was damp and combed, his blue T-shirt and shorts looked fresh from the dryer . . . and did I smell cologne?

I glanced down at my soccer shorts and tank top. The most I'd done was a side-of-my-head ponytail and a solid tooth brushing. But hey, no matter how good Tristan looked (and smelled), this was *not* a date.

So why was my blood throbbing like the time Chrissandra had challenged me to guzzle a can of Red Bull?

Leading him into the living room, I rolled my neck to try to ease some tension. But I knew that the best way to overcome anxiety was to put the "unknown" behind me. So I decided to turn and smack him on the lips. Just to get it over with.

Which would have been all well and good had he still been behind me and not stopped some feet back, head tilted as he scanned an open spiral notebook in his hand.

I unpuckered my mouth and cleared my throat.

He glanced up with that dark blue stare. "Oh, this? Last night I wrote down everything I could remember from camp."

Okay—that was impressive. Flattering, even, that he was taking this whole thing so seriously and not just going along with it for the "paycheck."

"Uh, thanks," I said. "So I guess you're the studious type, huh? You make the honor roll and all?"

"Not really. But when I care about something, I give it my all."

Everything inside me went tight, and I plopped down on the couch so hard that I bounced.

He closed the gap between us in a couple of long strides and sat down on the cushion beside me. "Okay, so first I was thinking we'd go over my notes—"

No way. First, we had to kill the tension. I reached out for his shoulders, and I pulled him toward me. Then

I pressed my sealed lips against his. In a kiss. Not a fly-me-to-the-moon kiss—but not a bad one, either.

Moments later, he shifted backward, breaking our seal.

"That," I said, attempting to explain, "was called . . . the Let's-Break-the-Ice Kiss."

His eyes seemed to do a slow dance across my face. "Or maybe it's the You-Want-Me-*That-Bad* Kiss."

I made a scoffing noise. "In your dreams."

"I don't know," he said in a rush of words. "I'm thinking I've been on your mind since we agreed to this last night, and you just couldn't wait to jump me."

I crossed my arms. "More like I wanted the antici-pation over."

"Anticipation? Of what? Being with me?" He huffed out a laugh. "Heck, I'm the one who has to perform here."

I instinctively opened my mouth to fire off some snappy comeback—but I found myself blank. I realized that he was right. The pressure *was* on him, for being the so-called pro. Why was I making this about me?

"Okay," I said, feeling a little stupid, "then take over, Coach."

A smile curved his lips. "I prefer the term Personal Trainer, if you don't mind."

I made a face. That sounded so . . . well, personal, and one-on-one, and, well, physical.

"Or sir."

"Sir!" *That* was too much. I raised a hand as if to swat him. "And I prefer Sparky."

He intercepted my hand in midair and laced his

fingers through mine. After a quick squeeze that startled my senses and blanked out my brain, he let go and thrust the notebook into my hand.

"Didn't you ever see that sign in the Greenfield cafeteria?" he asked, referring to the middle school. " 'The dictionary is the only place where *success* comes before *work*.' "

"Oh, puh-lease!" Part of me wanted to tease him for the mere mention of our middle school, but the simple truth was, we were wasting time. I wasn't going to get any closer to impressing Luke until Tristan and I got down to business.

And no matter how frustrated I got with him, I had to keep one simple thing in mind: if I didn't learn how to kiss, I could kiss my chances of varsity away.

It turned out Tristan was a man with a plan. He wanted to conquer the other parts of the face before the mouth. Namely, by refining the Caterpillar Kiss (the strange eyebrow messer), learning the proper etiquette of the Butterfly Kiss (entwining eyelashes) and the Eskimo Kiss (rubbing noses) and perfecting the Cheek Kiss (classic lips-to-cheek, of course).

It was *way* more fun than any classes I'd ever taken, especially since there were no rules against talking or breaking into laughter now and then. But I was surprised by how tiring it could be, and after a while, my facial muscles got sore and my mind started to wander.

Around ten, we took a break. After knocking back a

couple of glasses of fruit punch (and wiping the red streaks from around our mouths), we resumed our positions on the couch. Where Tristan announced that it was time to work on the lean-in.

"The side of the face you choose to approach your partner with actually tells volumes about how you feel about the person," he explained.

Who knew?

By the time he stood to leave for his water polo scrimmage, the only mouth-to-mouth action we'd shared was that stolen kiss when he'd first sat down.

I didn't know whether to feel disappointed or triumphant.

"So," I said, walking him to the door, "tonight, then? I'll get my mom's car and we'll find someplace to go." *Someplace dark,* I added silently. *Alone. Where no one will see us.*

"Sounds good."

Then it occurred to me: it was Friday night. We both knew nothing better would come along for *me*—unless Chrissandra had a change of heart. But I had to assume that Tristan had a life. "Unless you get a better offer," I added.

"Nah," he said, turning back. "You're top priority right now." A smile grazed his mouth, then rose to his eyes.

I was studying those eyes—wondering if navy blue properly described them—when they moved steadily closer. Before I knew it, his mouth was over mine, and

I'd lost my sense of sight. Probably because I'd closed my eyes when his tongue slid between my lips.

His hand cupping the back of my neck, I leaned deeper into the kiss, trying to study and feel and experience every aspect, every nuance.

Then suddenly he pulled away, taking my breath with him.

"That," he said, and grinned, "was the See-You-Later Kiss."

My hands fled to my upper arms, almost as if I was hugging myself. I couldn't help but think that a better name for that kiss might be the Leave-Them-Wanting-More Kiss. I waved him through the door, stunned into silence.

And then tried *not* to think about how incredibly delicious and delightful the kiss had been. And how my first French kiss had come from the freshman across the street.

Graduation: For many girls, great kissing is a diploma in itself; for many guys, it's a prerequisite to a bigger course of study.

That afternoon I pocketed the debit card my mom had left out for me and headed toward Old Town, intending to take full advantage of the one good thing about not quitting soccer altogether: shopping.

Waiting for the gates of the harbor bridge to lift, I was filled with a sort of bubbly excitement, the familiar and wonderful feeling that with the right outfit, anything is possible.

But it wasn't sweaters or jeans or jackets that were filling my brain. Strangely, it was the doorway kiss. Being mouth to mouth with Tristan had been, well, remarkable. A whole new experience. Which, when I stopped to analyze it, drove home my suspicion that my ex had been a dud in the kissing department.

But to keep things in perspective, I knew it wasn't the boy or the up-close action that I'd liked, as much as it was what that kiss had signified: hope.

The bell in the doorway tinkled when I entered Anna Banana's, and I made a beeline to a colorful table of V-necked sweaters, thinking how great they might look with a T-shirt underneath.

A momlike voice broke me from my musing. "Parker?"

I looked up to see Anna herself, dressed in her customary airy gauze clothing and too many necklaces.

"Looking for a back-to-school outfit?" she asked, her German accent so watered down from years in the U.S. that all that remained were some harder-than-usual syllables.

I nodded. "I kinda have my eye on that gray skirt in the window."

"Oh—oh . . . on *you*? Perfect! You've got the long legs to pull it off." She took me by the shoulders and turned me until I faced a dressing-room door. "You—there. Me—right back with everything in your size."

I let out a laugh and followed her instructions. Anna was great. And it had been a while since I'd gotten a compliment. Chrissandra had this theory that truly confident people—like we were supposed to be—didn't need the gratuitous support of others. That we could stand on our own two feet. And she felt that *some* compliments were actually backhanded insults, meant to demean previous outfits or hairstyles or other friends.

Her philosophy seemed a real stretch to me, maybe even a little paranoid, but rather than rock the Chrissandra boat, I'd learned to bite my tongue when she or Elaine wore something new or Mandy did some new streak in her hair. And to sort of frown at people and wave my hand dismissively if they said nice things about my looks in Chrissandra's presence.

Of course, with Chrissandra snubbing me, all that had changed. And how raw was the irony that now I didn't even have friends to trade compliments *with*?

Anna came back with a huge pile of clothes, including some long-sleeved tees that she swore would "make any day special." I loved her attitude, not to mention most everything she had me try on. Seeing the cash-register total, on the other hand, made me feel a little sick, but I punched in my mother's PIN, knowing she was cool about my clothing allowance. I figured it was payment for forcing me to "accept" the JV position.

I grabbed my receipt and was just turning to leave when I had a near collision—with Becca. I was hardly surprised to see her. She was, after all, an Anna Banana junkie, too. But I was surprised to almost knock her over and hoped my fancy-seeing-you-here expression thawed any ice.

"You're the last person I expected to see," she said, neither smiling nor frowning, showing not much of anything.

"Why? I shop here all the time."

"I mean, *now*. Chrissandra and some people are across the way, headed into the new Matt Damon movie."

The world spun before my eyes. Rationally, I knew my friends' lives hadn't stopped. I'd figured that phone calls and text and instant messages were firing around DeGroot, connecting people with plans that did not include me. But what I hadn't known for sure hadn't hurt me.

Now I knew.

And wow, it hurt.

"Why aren't you with them?" she asked.

I shifted my weight from one foot to the other. The truth seemed too easy—and yet too hard. And I had no idea how she'd react. I mean, sure, we used to have that unconditional BFF thing going on, but that was back when my idea of a great summer day was a blue raspberry slushy after a bike ride to the east side of the lake.

So, out of desperation, I did what any self-respecting loser would do: I laughed. And added an "Oh, yeah, well . . . ," which could have meant anything from *I'm totally over Matt Damon* to *I am an alien just visiting this planet in the body of Parker Stanhope.*

Becca studied my face. "You guys have a falling-out?"

"No!" I said, then paused, wishing I could recall my too-loud yelp. "No. I mean, not *really*. Okay, there's this little issue of me not getting promoted to varsity. You know," I said, like she or anyone would have a clue how dig-a-hole-in-the-ground humiliating it felt, "a temporary problem until Coach finds a place for me on varsity."

"Temporary."

"Totally. Over before you know it." If I lived that long. I shuffled my feet again. "Um, so, I guess I'll see you at school."

"You keep saying that."

"What?"

" 'See you at school.' "

I shook my head. "What? You won't be there?"

"I will. It's just, well, it's not like we really *see* each other there."

Huh? Couldn't she tell that this was no time to split hairs? Didn't she see that I was dying here?

I must have looked pissed or confused or something, because Becca shrugged, flashed something close to a smile and walked away.

I cruised on through the doorway, dragging my spirits and my chin behind me on the ground.

Outside, I headed toward home—not about to go anywhere *near* the movie theater. Wondering if I was still on Chrissandra's speed dial and in Mandy's and Elaine's Top Five. And if any of them had even once stopped to put themselves in my shoes, to try to imagine what I was going through and how it would have felt if the world had continued rotating without them.

But of course, I thought, it wouldn't have been one of them. Mandy and Elaine were the stuff college soccer scholarships were made of. And even though

Chrissandra had gotten in Hartley's face a few times as JV captain, she could practically kick a ball into the solar system. I was a solid player, but with Legs of Steel Rachael returning and that new girl transferring in, solid just wasn't enough.

Until now, our fearsome foursome had had nothing to do with talent and positions and everything to do with heart and trust and, well, loyalty. We were *there* together, *with* each other, *for* each other. Friends to the end.

I thought.

My breath caught in my throat as it really sank in for the first time. Was this the end? Like a ref giving me a red card that took me out of the game . . . forever?

Hand Kiss: This gesture of extreme politeness is considered totally impolite to refuse.

Clayton called that evening to check up on me. The mere sound of my brother's voice lifted me up, and I tried to sound sincere as I lied and said I had a handle on everything.

"Your coach doesn't know who she's tangling with," he said, and chuckled.

I made noises of agreement, thinking how glad I was to have him (and Luke) on my side.

We hung up, and I tried to copy a charcoal-eye-shadow look from a fashion magazine; then I went downstairs to borrow my mom's SUV for the next lesson.

Minutes later, Tristan and I were speeding off, his jaw clenched over "words" he'd just had with his dad.

"It was nothing," he said, and exhaled.

When I'd walked over to get him, he and his father had been arguing in the open garage.

"Is it because I'm older and therefore automatically a bad influence? Or because I'm my father's daughter?" I asked playfully.

He shot me an ice-cold glare, real electric blue, like wild-berry Gatorade.

"Wait—it *was* about me?" Unbelievable. Like I was social outcast number one.

"So what if it was?" He turned on the radio, but my mother kept the volume set so low that we didn't have to raise our voices. "Besides, he's got his own issues. Like why he won't get out of the car when he drops me at my mom's. Or the fact that he's involved in this nonsense with your dad."

"Well, that second part is easy," I said, braking for a traffic light. "He made that first call, after all."

"But he didn't. When he finally *did* decide to report something, it took him forever to even figure out how. I was there."

I found it hard to believe that Mr. Murphy wasn't the instigator. Who else would it be? We only had a neighbor on one side, and Mrs. Logan was almost too old to be alive, and practically blind. The rest of the people on Millard Circle kept to themselves and/or had lives.

"Well, however it got started," I said, "our dads have

certainly gone bonkers. They think they hate each other, but they seem like twins separated at birth."

"Which would make us cousins, you know. And make our deal illegal in quite a few states."

I made a face. "Don't even go there." I reached out and changed the radio station, turned up the volume and headed on to the scenic drive north.

After a time, the houses became farther and farther apart, until they all but disappeared. Finally, I pulled onto a dusty old road that led to a rocky bluff overlooking Lake Superior. I liked to think of it as my place, a little-known spot I'd discovered as a kid for picnicking and skipping rocks. My parents and Clayton had forgotten all about it, but after I'd gotten my driver's license, I'd brought Chrissandra, Elaine and Mandy out a few times. And after the varsity names were posted, this was where I'd come to cry.

Somehow it just seemed fitting to bring Tristan here, since he was—I prayed—the key to turning my life back around.

I killed the engine, and we got out. The night was dark and cool, the only light coming from the full moon, the only heat from, well, us.

Tristan moved to the lone wooden picnic table, then hopped up and sat, resting his feet on the bench. That's when I realized he was *sans* his trusty notebook.

"What? No notes tonight?"

He tapped his forehead. "It's all up here. And," he said, and lifted his hands, "right here."

Something stirred inside me.

But this was no time for self-analysis, so I climbed up and scooted close, until my thigh practically touched his. Crickets chirped everywhere—the bushes, the brush, the trees, more like a movie sound track than real life—and heightened my senses and anticipation.

He reached for my face with both hands, settling in with a palm on the side of my chin, his fingers splayed on my cheeks.

"The face hold," he said, "helps the kisser establish both interest and control, signaling his intentions to the kissee. The kissee then has the choice of backing away or holding still and waiting for the next move." His voice dropped, as did his hands. "Now your turn."

Dutiful student, I raised my hands and molded them to his face, much as he'd done. His skin felt warm, and smooth in some places, rough and stubbly in others.

"Now make your advance," he said, "until our lips touch."

I did, expecting the brush of our lips to take us someplace fabulous, or at least to deepen into, well, something. But as soon as we made contact, he pulled away.

"That was good. Now start again." My frown must have been evident in the moonlight, because he made a noise in the back of his throat. "Hey, you want to get this right or not? This could be a critical part of your performance at the sports fair."

He was right. Again. Still, I arched a brow to remind him to be respectful to his elders. But just as I was about to put him in his place, my words and thoughts were stolen by the sound of an approaching engine.

Leaping up, I spotted headlights out on the road. I hopped off the table, half figuring I'd creep through the brush to get a better look and half planning to stay there to keep from getting caught with Tristan.

The car lights were definitely getting brighter and bigger and seemed to slow, then to beam straight on me as the car braked on the bluff.

I tensed, panicky. I mean, I knew we hadn't done anything wrong, anything illegal. And anyone could be behind those lights: tourists, park patrol, grown-ups I'd never met. It didn't *have* to be a fate worse than death, right?

But the thing was, this was no hot spot. Especially at night. You almost had to know how to find it.

"Parker?" a male voice called out of the driver's-side window. "Is that you?"

Struggling to shield my eyes from the headlights, I scrambled to place the voice. "Uh," I managed, "yeah. Who's there?"

The driver's-side door popped open, and a lanky figure climbed out. After he'd taken a couple of steps, I recognized the strutting gait as Kyle Fenske's.

Chrissandra's Kyle.

Omigod. Did that mean *she* was behind those interrogation lights, too? Could this *get* any worse? I would probably have preferred my chances with an ax murderer.

"Hey," Kyle said, coming out in front of the lights.

"What are you doing out here? All alone at night and everything?"

Alone? My gaze swept from his to the picnic table.

Empty.

If it was possible to love someone two grades behind you, I suddenly did.

I zapped my focus back to Kyle. "I—I came out here after dinner to sort of clear my head. Things have been," I said, and swallowed hard, "sort of exhausting lately."

He nodded. He knew. *Of course* he knew. Chrissandra liked to talk.

"You have a car here, right? I mean, I'd give you a ride home and everything, but . . ."

"No, I'm good." Kyle always had been nice to me—even before he was dating Chrissandra, he'd offered me rides. I smiled at him and did my best to be casual. "I was just leaving, anyway," I said, and forced out a laugh. Before he could stop me, I scurried in the direction of the parked SUV. "See ya," I called back.

As I walked by, I peered into the dark interior of his car.

The passenger seat was empty, so either Kyle was here alone—or he was meeting someone. (Or someone was hiding from me?)

I jumped into the driver's seat of my mom's SUV, hoping to find Tristan hunkered down in the back, but no such luck. I started the engine, backed up and did a U-turn to head back to the road, driving little-old-lady slow, looking at every bush and tree. Finally, close to the main road, Tristan jumped out of some brush. Everything sort of warmed inside me, like when you first saw your cat that hadn't come home the night before.

I braked, and he climbed in beside me. I didn't even wait for him to put on his seat belt. I gunned it.

"You were great," I said. "Kyle never saw you."

"Who was that guy?"

"Chrissandra's boyfriend. Oh, Chrissandra is—"

"I know her name. I don't even go to DHS yet, but I've heard of her."

"So, yeah, you understand why it was critical that she didn't see us together. Or hear about it."

Gravel crunched under the tires as I slowed to a stop at the lip of the main highway. Another set of headlights appeared from the direction of DeGroot, turned toward us and cruised on in.

The car's headlights highlighted our faces before moving on, giving us one good look at the person behind the wheel.

One very familiar, very popular and very shocked Chrissandra Hickey.

I was screwed.

Improvement: Your kissing technique will benefit from practice—try running your tongue along your lips when no one is looking.

I don't think I slept that night. Okay, there were some moments where the edges of reality went fuzzy, but the usual trappings of comfort, escape and rest were nowhere near my twin bed.

Basically, I couldn't shrink from the fear that Chrissandra had seen Tristan and me and that it would change everything. That I'd stepped over her no-turning-back line and therefore was now unworthy of her trust and friendship. That I'd be eternally banished, to join the people susceptible to her vacant looks, dismissive shrugs or, worse, her incessant teasing.

Grasping at the hope that I could still wriggle my way

out, I worked up excuses about why Tristan was in my car, some far-fetched and some that hinged on sane. When the light finally seeped in around my drapes, it was gray and thick—a perfect accessory for the sleep-deprivation headache I now had. It seemed a lot easier to hide under the covers than to go downstairs and risk the hell of facing this day.

To my shock, I didn't get a single call or text message that day, or the next. And I admit to deciding that no news was good news. That somehow, Tristan and I had dodged a bullet.

Since he got bogged down by a day at his mom's, it wasn't until Sunday night—with the clock ticking toward the first day of school—that we were able to meet up again.

I told my parents I needed to take a walk to clear my head for school. And that's pretty much what I did. Just not alone.

Strolling toward the harbor, passing the usual twilight joggers and dog walkers, Tristan and I kept a respectable distance from each other. We were both well aware that, despite our lip locks, this was just business. We didn't need to be close, to touch, to connect. We just needed to get our stories straight, and figure out how to best spin them.

"Okay," I told him, breaking the silence. "You accidentally left the wristwatch your mom gave you for eighth-grade promotion out on the shore. And you paid me to drive you back there to get it."

"I don't wear a watch."

I shrugged. "Well, *yeah*. Not anymore. Because we couldn't find it."

He looked unconvinced. "How about you're teaching me to drive?"

"Do you even have your learner's permit?"

"No. Which is why we went out to a remote part of the lake."

"In the dark?"

"We got a late start."

"Hmmm . . . not bad," I said, wrinkling my nose in consideration. "But we gotta say you're paying me. Like you came to me this summer and we negotiated the deal."

"Twenty bucks a session."

"Twenty-five," I said, just to be ornery.

A grin touched his mouth. "You take cash?"

"Only unmarked bills."

We got to a bench and sat down. "The good news," I went on, "is that I didn't get any calls this weekend asking about you. Making me think . . . hope . . . wish that somehow Chrissandra only saw *me*. And that if she mentioned me to Kyle, he said I was alone."

"Maybe," Tristan said, but his frown told me his heart wasn't in his answer.

"People's eyes naturally go to the driver first; plus, she *was* driving kind of fast."

"Yeah, but at six feet, a person's kind of hard to miss at any speed."

"You're not *that* big—"

"What—you think that because I'm a freshman, I'm automatically invisible?"

I let out a little laugh. "Yeah, that's it." I nodded toward a lady walking a beagle. "Like right now, she thinks I'm wacko and talking to myself."

He rolled his eyes, but a smile snuck through.

"To keep things safe until we know what Chrissandra saw," I went on, "don't come by my locker or say anything to me at school until I make the first move, okay?"

He paused, then did this exaggerated bow, which made me uncomfortable on a number of levels, one of which was the fact that it called attention to us. "Oh, yes, madam, I am to maintain the lowest of profiles."

"That's right, Sparky."

He frowned. "Okay, but when you work things out with your friends and finally *do* recognize me, I want it to be good. Like a big hug. And then you have to add something like if only I was a couple grades ahead, you'd totally jump my bones."

"*What?*"

"Well, wouldn't you?"

"Jump your bones? No way!"

"You mean you haven't liked these lessons, even a little bit?"

I crossed my arms. "It's work."

"Along the lines of cleaning the latrine at summer camp or SAT prep?"

He had me there. "Not *that* bad."

"Okay, then."

"Okay," I said, not sure exactly what was okay or what we'd agreed on but knowing I owed him some kind of compromise. And the fact that I had no friends to share the news of his so-called hotness with pretty much took care of my end of the deal.

Morning came all too soon, and with it, the start of my junior year.

Cruising the halls in my first-day-of-school finest—which I prayed covered my quaking knees and camouflaged my sweating armpits—I felt that sort of light-headedness that comes from running too hard. But instead of giving me the certainty that all would be normal again once I caught my breath, my gut told me things were going to get way worse before they ever got better.

Amazingly, I made it to my locker without incident. CeeCee Stevens, who for the third year in a row had the locker to my right, turned and smiled. She tended to reinvent herself every few months—a new hair color, tattoo or piercing, and for her last birthday, perky new boobs—but the one thing that stayed the same was the gap between her two front teeth.

"Hey, Parker. Have a good summer?"

I wanted to scoff, to tell her that I'd endured countless hot, humid soccer practices, only to end up like the ball itself, kicked offsides. But I kept my head and simply nodded and asked about hers.

"Not bad," she said, "other than an unbearable family vacation that ended with me nearly jumping out of our van in the wilds of Wisconsin in order to hitchhike home."

I managed a smile, relieved that she thought I could relate to pain-in-the-butt relatives being the worst of a girl's problems. When I was enduring the worst possible pain—being cast off by my friends.

Inside my first-period class, Español Tres, I chatted with a couple of guys I'd known since sandbox days. Then a girl from my last year's Spanish class plopped down beside me—giving me the impression once again that someone was happy to see me.

I tried to smile back, but I'm pretty sure all I did was stare. At her, at the two guys and around the room. I mean, was I missing something?

I quickly took inventory:

I was the athletic girl whose skills had been put to the test and then had been ruled substandard.

I was the popular girl who'd been shunned by her popular crowd.

I was an eleventh grader who'd almost/sorta (oh, God, I hoped not) been caught in a compromising position with a ninth grader.

Why weren't they giggling and staring?

If this had happened to someone last year, Chrissandra would have been on this like white on rice, making up sidesplitting jokes and encouraging Elaine, Mandy and me to one-up her. All in good fun, of course—but maybe not so great to the one being made fun of.

Was it possible that I'd misunderstood the speed of gossip? That no one knew yet? Had I been overruled by the news of some hot hookup or breakup?

The thought was almost too good to be true, but I was anxious to find out. While Señora Trujillo took attendance, I decided to tempt fate. I leaned toward the girl beside me casually and whispered, "Did you hear Rachael Washington came back to soccer and basically took my varsity spot?"

She lifted her brow. "Yeah. Sorry. But you'll make it next year." A tinge of sympathy crossed her face, but then she looked back at the teacher, who was now reading off *S* surnames.

"Parker Stanhope?" Señora Trujillo called out, interrupting my confusion.

"¡Aquí!" I answered, then threw an anxious glance around the classroom. Nope, not one snicker, not one craned neck, not even a curious glance.

I was just . . . regular old me. Not a freak of nature, not socially nonexistent—not worth gossiping over. It was like people couldn't care less if I played on JV or varsity. If I had friends or not. It was like I didn't matter.

And I wasn't sure if that was a good sign or not.

I got through my first few classes in a daze. Mandy waved to me from the other side of the room in chem, and I got the feeling from the upward tilt of her nose that she was quite happy we'd all been seated alphabetically, so that she didn't have to deal with the quandary of whether to be seen talking to me.

Needless to say, I was super-surprised to find her waiting for me in the doorway after class. Although her innocent looks were usually weighed down by heavy streaks of blue hair dye and eye shadow, her baby face still made her look like someone your mother would let you stay out late with. I knew—from experience.

"You're . . . okay, I hope," she said with a concerned frown.

I managed a nod while studying her eyes, wondering why she was letting herself be seen with me. Was she breaking ranks? Could I have a true friend in her after all?

We fell into step together with the rest of the lunch crowd, toward the junior-class corridor.

"You know, I think it sucks that you didn't make varsity," Mandy suddenly said.

I swallowed and nodded—not a comfortable combo—and we rounded the corner to my locker. I dug for a response but came up empty.

"You're such a great player, Parker. Like that goal against Cleveland last year . . ."

My gaze traveled a few feet—to see Chrissandra and Elaine and a couple of other girls from last year's JV team huddled in front of a locker.

My locker.

Chrissandra looked me straight in the eye and

beamed, her bright blue eyes glowing. Kyle's letterman jacket hung almost to the hem of her frayed jean shorts, with the lowest snaps closed. I knew she thought this look made her legs look longer and sleeker, but the opposite was closer to the truth. Though there wasn't a person at D.H.S. who'd dare tell her.

"Surprise!" she announced, then led a group step-away.

My insides warmed, like seeing the ball you just kicked get past the goalie into the net. Surely my locker would be decorated with bows and heart-shaped Post-its, like we'd occasionally done to celebrate birthdays and game-winning plays. Surely they'd decided to take me back—okay, surely Chrissandra had—and to stand by me through thick or thin.

Maybe Luke and I wouldn't even have to go through with our kissing-booth charade.

The last girl moved away. But nothing sparkly or Day-Glo or eye-catching jumped out on my locker at all. Just something dangling from a string from my vent.

I took a step closer, everything inside me tightening.

A pacifier.

Like you'd give to a baby. If you happened to have one in your family. Or as your new boyfriend.

Jawbreaker: There's just nothing better than a kiss that uses every last facial muscle.

"We figured a pacifier was *just* what you needed, Parker," Chrissandra asserted, her eyes still gleaming. "Seeing as how you're dating a baby."

The world spun before me, like in those first few moments of a Google Earth search. From somewhere—the West Indies or New Zealand or hell—came a chorus of laughter.

And while I told myself that this was all an act—Chrissandra had warned me that they'd be coming off as bitches—I also knew the game had changed a lot since that phone conversation. I'd been caught with a freshman. And that was the ultimate deal breaker.

"No," I said emphatically, "I don't like him like that."

"Like what?" Chrissandra said. "Clothed?"

The girls laughed.

"Oooh, Parker!" Elaine cried "You need ice for that burn!"

I ignored them, keeping my gaze on our fair leader. "It's not what you think."

"Oh?" she said, arching a brow, an expression I knew meant that her opponent was about to become toast. "So tell me, mind reader. What *do* I think?"

Crap! Chrissandra 3, Parker o. Experience told me this was going to be a total blowout. All I could do was keep my cool—and some moisture in my mouth. If I'd learned anything these past couple of weeks, it was that ultimately, I would survive. Maybe not in a fantabulous way, but I knew I could at least stay on my feet.

Chrissandra's face took on a triumphant look, one she shared with the group. "You *don't* know what I'm thinking, do you? How could you? You're like a froshie again yourself: playing on JV, dating one."

"Yeah," Mandy said, "it's like they're going to have to take you out of the yearbook."

"*Cut* her out," Chrissandra corrected. "Of the last *two* yearbooks. And put her picture in this year's freshman pages."

"Uh, yeah," Mandy said, clearly remembering the script now. "It's like you never existed."

Again, titters and giggles.

"I'll spell out exactly what I am thinking," Chrissandra

said, hand on hip. "I saw you with that *boy*. I know what you were doing out at the lake with him because I was there to do the same thing with Kyle."

This was bad. Superbad. Killer bad. So bad that *bad* needed a new name.

For lack of a response, I plucked the pacifier from my locker and balled it in my hand. Denial, at this point, was a waste of my breath. I could go with the driving-lessons thing, but it suddenly seemed so lame, I wasn't even sure I could say it with a straight face. My only out was the truth, the kissing-booth plan, but how could I admit to moving ahead on something that only worked if one of the varsity players—maybe one of them—got thrown off the team?

Of course, the way I was feeling, I hardly cared if they all got their butts kicked off.

I was lost in Loserville. If I couldn't deny it, and I couldn't fess up, what was left? Tears? Begging for forgiveness? Accepting banishment? Or . . . how about wowing Chrissandra with an imitation of her idol, Juliet Capulet; doing some dramatic oration in iambic pentameter, one that probably amounted to absolutely nothing but sounded so good you couldn't help listening? In other words, coming back at her with some really elaborate BS.

And then it struck me, as bald-faced as one of Tristan's kisses: *Romeo and Juliet*. That was it. The only way out of this was to be tragic. It was a big gamble but worth a shot.

I inhaled for strength, then glanced down, willing tears to fill my eyes. "Okay—you've got me. It's one of those things," I managed, keeping my head averted. "I know it's wrong, but it just feels right. I know, I'm two grades ahead of him, and I'm smarter and I'm more popular. Plus, I have way cooler friends," I threw in for good measure. "And can you believe our dads are in a total feud that's practically coming down to crossed swords in the street?"

I glanced up, right at Chrissandra. "But he *is* only a year younger, and he's totally buff, and he's got these awesome dark blue eyes." (If you were into dark blue eyes.) "And, you know, you just can't control what the heart wants. So yeah, go ahead and make fun of me if you want. But it'll never change the fact that I'm head over heels in love with Tristan Murphy."

Did I really just say that?

I held Chrissandra's gaze. My blood thrummed in my ears. Time stood still.

"Omigod, Park," she finally said, her voice cracking. "That is *so* Leonardo and Claire." She took a couple of steps toward me and threw her arms around my neck.

I returned the hug, feeling both triumphant and superiorly manipulative.

"I am so happy for you," she gushed, then pulled back and brushed some of my hair from my cheek. "I mean, Kyle and I are *good,* and Elaine had that hot thing going with what's-his-name last year, but you're the first of our group to find her soul mate, the guy she'd live and die for."

Elaine, Mandy and the other two girls took the cue and moved in for a group hug, which was so cute and sweet that it made my teeth hurt. But hey, you didn't see me complaining. Sure, I had the trial now of a supposed boyfriend of the inferior class, who I did not want, but much more important, I was winning the war.

"It's like it was written in the stars," Chrissandra went on. "I'll bet Tristan was the reason you didn't make varsity to begin with, so you could fit completely into his life."

My jaw (and my hopes) dropped. "No! I didn't make varsity because of Rachael and that new girl. He—he came later. I was, uh, teaching him how to drive," I said, nonsensical, desperate words tumbling out of my mouth, "and it just happened."

Chrissandra narrowed her eyes. "You mean to tell me, after meeting your other half, you don't believe in destiny?"

I ran my gaze from face to face, although I knew it was no use soliciting the help of the crowd. No one would side against their queen bee.

"Of course I believe in destiny," I managed. "But—"

"No buts," she said, letting me know I'd effectively nailed my own coffin shut. "We're absolutely thrilled for you, Parker." She threw a look at Elaine.

"Jealous, even." Elaine added. "In a weird way."

Chrissandra nodded. I could almost count the beats until Mandy said something in agreement.

"Yeah," Mandy said.

The other two parrots nodded.

"But your romance with this froshie," Chrissandra said, taking the reins again, "just tells us you're where you need to be. I'm sure you'll make lots of new friends. I'll bet the frosh and soph girls will totally look up to you. You'll probably even be named team captain. This time."

Okay, that was below the belt. Meaner than mean and uncalled-for. Someone had mentioned me for JV captain last year, but, of course, Hartley had given the honor to Chrissandra. Why bring that up? And how could she even remember something like that at a time like this?

But, the thing was, I was fighting for my life here. "Look, I can't control what Hartley did. But I'll tell you, I'd *much* rather be with you guys than the JV girls—and if it means quitting soccer altogether, well, then I'll do that."

The girls drew spontaneous gasps, while a slow smile crept over Chrissandra's face. She'd heard this threat from me in our "secret" conversation, although she couldn't admit it.

"Your call, Parker," she said. "Whatever you want. But I don't even see why we're discussing this. You've got the love of your life now—what else do you need?"

She turned away, and her subordinates followed. Leaving me feeling stripped naked and vulnerable. And losing-a-game-by-one-goal furious.

Part of me wanted to chase after them and tell them all where to shove it. I hated them! How *dared* they reject me, or decide what was best for me?

But then something was telling me that there was more going on than met the eye and that if—no, *when* we worked this whole thing out, we'd all be better friends for it.

I had to stand tall. Firm. Silent. This was not over. It was just another detour on the road back to Happily Ever After. Because the Plan was still in place. And it would work. It would! But right now, I needed to get over to the cafeteria and get some carbs and protein in me so I didn't pass out at practice later.

Oh, and last but not least? I had to chase down Tristan and let him know we were madly, passionately and tragically in love.

Kiss and Tell: Whether you're kissing to show affection, say hello or say goodbye, give your best and you won't be sorry.

I couldn't find Tristan in the cafeteria or out in the courtyard, which made me wonder whether freshmen really *were* invisible. As the day wore on, I got more and more anxious about tracking him down. The guy needed to be clued in to his grand love for me.

After last bell, figuring Heartless owed me at least one favor, I poked my head into her office and announced I'd be a few minutes late for practice. I ducked out before she had a chance to answer. What was she going to do—throw me off the team?

Traveling through the corridors and then outside. I

scanned the various groups for a tall freshman. And after several frustrating and fruitless minutes, I all but gave up. Then, as I was turning back toward the building, he was suddenly right across from me, sitting on a low wall with some buddies. His slightly averted eyes told me he'd seen me, too, but was playing by our rules—okay, *my* rules.

My mind raced. Should I call him away? Go act all friendly, as if I talked to people like him every day? Or . . . hmmm. Since thinking before acting hadn't been winning me any awards, why not do something spontaneous?

"There you are." I waited until I had his attention, stepped closer, then slid in close to him.

Tristan smiled brightly as his eyes widened in surprise, accenting his dark, long lashes. After a long moment, his gaze moved from mine to his circle of friends, then back to my gaze again.

"Parker . . . ," he said in an urgent half whisper, like there might still be time for me to untangle myself and preserve my rep.

I looped my arms around his neck, which was wider and firmer than I remembered, and a little sweaty, too. "It's okay, babe," I said with a big play-along-with-me smile. "We've been outed. Everyone knows we're together, and it's cool."

"Cool?"

"Yes—cool." To drive my point home, I leaned in and kissed him. Smack on the lips. Not with the skill he'd shown me recently, but still not half bad, if I said so myself. Pulling back, I saw the question marks in his eyes.

I totally had explaining to do, but for now, job done. "Listen, I'm late for practice. Talk to you tonight?"

Tristan stood and took a step toward me, as if to follow. "Without a doubt."

I turned and, as naturally as possible, walked away, chuckling, but not walking so fast or chuckling so loud that I missed the whoops and cheers from the guys in his crowd. Suffice it to say, I'd paid my debt. In spades.

Coach Hartley, on the other hand, was not so agreeable. After calling me into her office, she did a head-shaking, sighing thing certainly intended to make me feel guilty.

"I understand you're not happy with me right now, Parker," she said, clearly not happy herself. "But we have team rules, and they start with being prompt and ready to play, remember?"

I pressed my lips together so that I didn't let out what I really wanted to say: how I'd always shown up on time, always been ready to play, and a fat lot of good *that* had done me.

"Remember?" she repeated.

It was my turn to sigh. "Yes, I remember."

Heartless moved to the door and called Lyric Wolensky in. I'd known Lyric since our first year here, and, while she was a decent goalie, her personality off the field was as dull as her mousy brown hair. She often got lost or forgotten in the chaotic chatter of the locker room, and when she did speak up, her top lip barely moved.

Coach settled back behind her desk after Lyric took the hard plastic chair beside me. "Girls, I know you both expected to make varsity. I had every intention of moving the whole team up. But it became a numbers game." She shrugged. "Please know it was tough for me to make those decisions and post that list."

I hugged myself so my heart didn't bleed all over her carpet.

"And know I've got big things planned for you this season. Leadership roles and inclusion in pivotal decisions. Next year, when you're seniors on varsity, if things have gone well, I'll see if I can extend those same privileges. So try not to look at this year as being held back as much as preparing you for great things next year."

I followed Lyric's lead of a weak smile, when all I could think was *Nice try, Heartless*.

"And of course, you are the first choices if a position should open this fall on varsity. So stay at the top of your game, set the right example for the younger players and be ready to lead the team to a championship."

Lyric thanked her, while I just nodded.

"At the end of practice today," Hartley went on, "I'll be naming you JV captain, Parker, and you," she said, looking at Lyric, "cocaptain. Start preparing a few words now, because after the applause, I know you'll want to speak." She grinned, like this public recognition and acknowledgment of our JV-ness was an honor.

Since my parents did raise me to have manners, I mumbled something to her that sounded grateful. Then I wandered out of her office, my mind all over Chrissandra's reaction, which I wagered would fall somewhere between an "I told you so" and a nose-in-the-air snub. I knew better than to expect sympathy and an invitation back into the fold.

In other words, Heartless had just given me the one kiss I was betting Tristan could never teach me: the kiss of death.

Lyric caught up to me. "So, captain and cocaptain," she said, her tone so flat, her face so frozen, that I didn't know if she was near tears or happier than she'd ever been in her life.

"Yeah," I muttered. "Whoop-de-do."

"Hey, at least you're top dog."

Sunlight smacked me when I pulled open the gym door. I waited until she'd joined me on the concrete, then turned back to her. "You want it, Lyric? It's yours."

Her brown hair bobbed with her head shake. "No thanks. I figure, as cocaptain, if there *is* an opening on varsity, she'll pick me first. I mean, why promote the captain and shake up both teams?"

I opened my mouth to laugh, to tell her she was absolutely right, but for some reason, no sound came out.

All I could think of was how hard I'd worked that morning to get up my nerve to come to school, how I'd convinced myself that effort and a good attitude would pay off. And while most people *had* basically accepted or ignored me, the few who'd paid me real attention had tromped soccer cleats on what was left of my life.

I guess it only stood to reason that my father chose that night to freak out over my "friendship" with Tristan.

Apparently he had seen the two of us drive off on Friday night. My mother told me she'd calmed him down by telling him that I was helping Tristan adjust to high school (which she believed to be true). While my father was decent enough to think it neighborly of me, he had definite lines where his niceness ended and his psychotic behavior began. And as far as he was concerned, I was fraternizing with the enemy.

After dinner, with Mom chatting away on the phone to Clayton, I made a general announcement into the air that I was going for a walk—and apparently crossed my dad's invisible line.

"With the Murphy boy again?" he asked, moving into the doorway in what could have been perceived as a block.

I shrugged. "Yeah. Does it matter? We're just, you know, talking about teachers and stuff." Stuff like Eskimo Kisses and lean-ins and how we're supposedly in love.

My dad's heavy brow (which seemed to get heavier with the mention of anything Murphy) lowered. "That's it?"

"That's it," I said, crossing my fingers at my side and wondering if eventually I'd have to—God forbid—spread the lie about our "romance" to my family, too.

"He doesn't ask you questions about . . . me, about the house?"

A laugh snaked its way up and out of me (probably not a good move, but you can't always control your reactions). "No. What, you think Tristan is working for his dad to get the goods on you so he can launch preemptive attacks?"

He glared at me.

"You think they're going to subpoena me in small-claims court," I went on, "to testify against you?"

"That is not funny, Parker."

Since my mother was still chatting away, I ignored the implied don't-stress-your-father-out rule and said exactly what I thought. "You're right, Dad. It's not funny. This whole thing between you and his father is *so* not funny it's embarrassing."

Tension clenched his jaw, telling me he was *not* saying way more than he *was* saying. "Well, if he does ask you anything suspicious, don't answer right away. Give me a chance to decide what to tell him."

Omigod, were we like that *Spy Kids* family now, all working together to bring down the enemy?

He glowered, then stepped away from the door. "And just don't you forget whose roof you live under."

How could I? It was the one with the gutters so meticulously painted that Mr. Murphy couldn't report us if he wanted to.

Spotting Tristan shooting baskets in the street moments later made my legs pick up speed. Finally—someone with no agenda, no rules, no hidden knives to slip into my back. I practically skipped down the driveway and across the street.

"Hey, stranger."

He bit back a smile, dribbling the ball. "Well, well, if it isn't the love of my life."

"Yeah. About *time* you realized the effect I have on you."

He rolled his midnight blue eyes, but a smile hung around his mouth. "I assume this all has to do with soccer and Chrissandra?"

"Don't all my roads lead there?" I let out a big breath and recounted what had happened by my locker and how I'd come to announce that we were victims of star-crossed love.

"Risky," he said when I was done. He rested the ball on the pavement and stopped it from rolling with the tip of his sneaker. "But good going."

"Well, I figured I had two things working for us. Agewise, you really should be a sophomore, which still isn't great, but better than a freshman."

"There's that."

"And you're . . . ," I said, and shrugged, "you know . . . okay-looking."

"Okay-looking?" he repeated, probably because he liked how it sounded.

"Sure," I said, then caught myself gazing past him. Funny, I couldn't begin to pinpoint when I'd stopped seeing a slightly annoying neighbor and started seeing someone worth looking at. "Well," I tried to clarify, "not

Luke Anderson, prom king, okay-looking. But, you know, as okay-looking as a guy in your grade can be."

"Thanks. I guess." He took a step closer. I could feel the warm puffs of his breath on my forehead.

"The way I figure it," I told him, "about the time I go off to college—when *you're* a junior—you'll totally be worth dating."

"Again, not sure if I should say thanks or not." His mouth pursed into a smile, not so easy to see at this close proximity—more something I could feel. "And until then, Parker, you'll, what, put up with me?"

I pulled back and looked dead into his face. I knew this was all in fun, but if I'd given him any indication that we had a future, well, I'd screwed up. "Yeah, Sparky, but not for long. The sports fair is a week from tomorrow, and I can't have people feeling sorry for you, thinking I'm cheating on you, when I'm doing a major make-out with Luke."

Something flickered and died in his eyes, like the last embers of a campfire. "So we'd better schedule a big breakup for this weekend, huh? Like at the Dairy Queen, where I storm off, leaving you sobbing in your Oreo Blizzard?"

"Sobbing," I grumbled. I reached out to playfully smack his formidable chest, but he caught my hand inside his two. And held it.

For a crazy moment, I thought he was going to pull all of me toward him and kiss me. And while I figured I'd like it (maybe even a lot), it just wouldn't be cool. Our kisses were either educational or to be used for show at school. And imagine if my dad peeked out the window and saw?

Speaking of Dad . . .

"Look, I really better go," I said, tugging my hand free.

"Yeah, me too." He took a step back. "So listen, now that we're a so-called couple, if I see you in the halls or whatever, I can come up to you and everything?"

"And everything," I said, and lifted my brow.

"Kiss you like the guy in *Titanic*?"

"Or like the guy in *Gone with the Wind*."

His eyes went dull.

"An old movie. Never mind. You have to be like, *my age* to have seen it."

He shook his head. Then he reached for his basketball. But instead of tucking it under an arm and heading home, he raised the ball over his head, lined up a shot and launched it. Into a perfect arc and swish.

Glad some people's lives are charmed.

Longevity: Remember, you're not out to set any records. Short kisses can be just as passionate as their longer counterparts.

Approaching my locker the next morning, I didn't know what to expect. But whether the girls had upped the ante in exploiting my "romance" or had already lost interest in it (and in me), the situation was total lose-lose.

I squinted as I rounded the corner, then opened my eyes fast. Discount coupons for diapers and baby wipes hung off "It's a Boy!" wrapping paper on my locker door. All that was missing was a video camera ready to capture my shame for viewing on HomeroomTV and YouTube.

"Cute," I grumbled to no one in particular. "Real cute."

The honey-skinned Rachael Washington caught my eye in passing. Her black hair pulled back tight off her face, she was all wide eyes and red-painted lips. "You think so? I think it's totally immature."

Pushing aside the fact that I couldn't remember the last time she had spoken to me—obviously this was a week to blaze new and strange trails—and the fact that she was basically the reason the varsity roster had closed without me, I went with her sentiment and rolled my eyes. "It's going to be way cuter in a thousand pieces on the floor."

She wriggled off her backpack. "Sounds fun. Can I play?"

I dug a nail under a loose corner of paper and ripped it in two across the center while she jumped in for her own noisy tear. We continued like sharp-clawed kittens until the paper and coupons lay in shreds.

"You were right," she said, glancing back up at me. "Much cuter. What's this all about, anyway? The ninth grader I hear you're dating?"

I nodded, not at all surprised. The only thing my "friends" passed faster than a soccer ball was gossip. "Yeah . . ."

"I hope he's worth it."

I tried to nod and smile, but mostly I think I just shrugged.

"Well, whatever," she said, and shrugged herself. "Listen, there's something I wanted to talk to you about."

All I could think was that she was going to apologize

for returning to soccer and ruining my life. Something Hallmark didn't make a card for. And while it wouldn't make things better, I would be all ears.

"We should do lunch one day this week," she said instead. "Compare strategies, make sure we're in sync with leading our teams."

As if the lunch offer weren't shocking enough, the "leading" part caused my lashes to fly back against my brows. My thoughts did a Rubik's Cube shuffle until they neatly lined up. "Hartley," I spoke, "chose you as varsity captain?" *And not Chrissandra?*

"You didn't hear?"

"As you can tell," I said, and gestured toward the scraps of wrapping paper on the ground, "I'm sort of out of the loop. But Chrissandra's your cocaptain, then?"

"No, I don't have a cocaptain."

That was impossible. The previous year's JV captain was *always* promoted to a varsity leadership position. But Rachael's stony face told me she wasn't kidding. So basically, she had come out of "retirement" to single-handedly lead varsity. Which was why she wanted to network with me. At least I had that question answered.

"How did Chrissandra take it? Getting passed over . . . for nobody."

"I honestly didn't notice." She lifted her backpack and slid it on. Something told me her silence spoke volumes, but this was not the time to go there. "Listen, is tomorrow good for you?"

"Sure." Tomorrow, or any day. It wasn't like I had a

group to sit with anymore. Unless you counted my JV teammates, which—duh—I didn't.

"Meet you here," she said, and turned to go, leaving a vaguely citrus scent in her wake, which must have come from her hair products, her body spray or the fact that she was just so amazingly perfect.

I focused on my lock—only to find my next-door locker neighbor, CeeCee, staring at me like I had two heads.

"Nice mess, Parker."

So much for idle chitchat about vacations and annoying families. "I'm going to clean it up. Don't worry."

"So is it true, then? That you're with a freshman?"

Ugh! I had just about reached my limit. I wanted to shout "No!" and spill the whole truth about Heartless and Luke and how I'd soon be back in business, but I managed a tiny nod instead.

"And that you two," she continued, "are *doing it*?"

"What?" I shrieked, horrified. "Who said that?" I demanded.

"People."

" 'People' are wrong."

She tilted her head. The overhead light sent a glimmer to her diamond nose ring. "Then what *are* you doing with him?"

I tried to swallow. "Uh . . . trying to make a relationship work."

Her forehead went all wrinkly. "That's crazy. You

could get any number of guys. Decent guys. Even hot guys. Like, doesn't Kyle Fenske have a thing for you?"

She was confusing me with Chrissandra—but no use going there.

"And I heard the guys' soccer team did high fives when you and your boyfriend broke up last spring."

Okay, *that* was just dumb. But kind of flattering, if it was true.

"I can't really explain it," I said, concentrating on my acting skills and looking just past her ear so she couldn't read the lie in my eyes. "But feelings this strong, this real, well, they're not something you can analyze or deny. Just something you have to go with, and see where they lead."

Like to being a laughingstock who would never get her friends back. Or, on the flip side, back to varsity and the life I once loved. With no in-between, no happy medium and no idea which way the pendulum would swing.

Was I crazy? Maybe. But mostly, I was without options.

The lines in CeeCee's forehead all of a sudden disappeared; then she let out a sigh. "Well, *whatever*, I guess. As long as you keep him and his friends away from here. I mean, I've got a rep to maintain."

I did, too. That's what this whole thing was about. But I couldn't say that, so I did what I could do: I bent down to clean the mess off the tile floor.

I'm pretty traditional about my meals (I get that from my dad, I suppose), going with your basic chicken fingers or pepperoni pizza for lunch. But I couldn't bring myself to wander friendlessly through the cafeteria that day, like a neon sign of loserness.

So I rustled up the change from the bottom of my backpack and hit the snack machines, going with honey-mustard-and-onion pretzels and a Cherry Coke for my stomach and a couple of white-iced Little Debbie snack cakes for my soul.

"I'm all about the fudge cakes myself," a voice said behind me.

I turned to see a beauty mark above a slightly smirking mouth. Becca's and my conversation from the other day dive-bombed back at me. "See?" I told her, and smiled. "We *do* see each other here at school."

"Yeah, well, what do you know?"

I backed away to give her space and watched as she clinked in a bunch of coins. Thinking that since she was here and I was here . . .

"Seems like maybe we should celebrate this chance meeting," I said, and forced out a laugh. "Sit down somewhere and scarf these things together."

Her dark eyes darted toward me, and while I wasn't quite sure what I was seeing in them, her nod told me she was up for killing a few minutes.

We wandered out the side door and sat down on a curb. Her skirt was short, and I wondered if the concrete scratched her legs, but the insistent way she tore at her

snack-cake package told me she was way more interested in her stomach than her legs.

"Cute skirt," I said, to fill the silence. And, you know,
because it was.

"Same one you have, just in blue."

I was about to argue, then took a closer look. Little
embroidered flowers, two front pleats—she was right.
I'd bought it at Anna Banana's last spring and worn it to
school a few times.

"No wonder I like it," I said awkwardly, then
crunched a pretzel. "And more proof that we see each
other at school. How else would you have known about
my skirt?"

She crammed the last hunk of a cake into her mouth
like she was pushing back a reply. I realized she probably just didn't want to admit she was wrong . . . and
tried to remember if that was why I'd stopped hanging
around with her after middle school.

But for now, we were sitting here, and I *was* grateful
for company. So I pressed on, asking about her older
sister and if she'd gone away to college.

"Yeah, she got into MIT. In fact, when I saw you in
the supermarket the other day, I'd only just gotten back
from saying goodbye to her at the airport."

I tried to remember if she'd had swollen eyes or had
seemed super-sad, but all I could remember was trying
to rush through so she wouldn't put two and two together
on my strange grocery haul.

"I've gotten better at goodbyes," she added. "Remember how emo I went at Alexis's goodbye party?"

My thoughts circled back to her eighth-grade water-works and all the snot and saliva she'd ended up slob-bering on my shoulder during a group hug. But it was kind of sweet, how sentimental Becca used to get.

"Yeah," I said, "and then, six months later, Alexis was back at school anyway." I smiled and nudged her.

"What a perfectly good waste of tears." She let out a thoughtful laugh. "And then there was how I sobbed at my grandmother's funeral."

"Yeah," I said, leaning in a bit, "but Becca, that was different."

"Yeah," she agreed.

I kind of wanted to hug her or pat her or something, but the bell rang, conveniently saving me from some display that would either embarrass or annoy her. There was no faking that we were friends like that anymore.

Standing, I brushed some crumbs off my shirt. Becca glanced down at her own shirt, then up at me.

"I'm here sometimes for lunch," she said, then shrugged. "Okay—I'm here a lot. If you ever . . ."

I nodded, happy to find someone not embarrassed to be seen with me. "Yeah. But hey, we gotta reach a lit-tle higher than grade-A junk. There's that grill truck that comes out front. Hamburgers and stuff. Maybe we should try that sometime."

"Yeah."

"Okay," I said, and grinned.

"Okay. Later, then."

"Later."

Becca took the stairs and I headed down the hall,

toward my locker. But when I came face to face with Chrissandra, Mandy and Elaine, I longed for the simplicity of those last, awkward moments with Becca.

I was still mad about the stuff on my locker (and everything else), but I knew I had to sideline those feelings. When things worked out—*when*—I'd find the right time and place to tell them how they'd hurt me. But that time was definitely not now.

So I reached into the same hidden reservoir of strength that had propelled me to drag Luke and Tristan into my plans, and smiled. "You guys were busy little bees this morning."

My gaze joined Elaine's and Mandy's in a straight shot to Chrissandra. Chrissandra looked right back at me.

"You're not mad?" she asked, then examined a fingernail.

"Mad?" I said, and forced out a laugh that had a moment of homeless-lady insanity. "No! I thought it was funny. In fact, Rachael and I had a good laugh while we peeled it off."

Chrissandra's brow arched. "Rachael?"

Bull's-eye. Just a suspicion, but I thought her name would rankle Chrissandra.

"Yeah, she came by to congratulate me on becoming JV captain." Holding my breath, I smiled again. "You were right, Chrissandra. Coach did lob that on me."

Mandy took a step forward. "And she made Rachael our captain. Which was just crazy."

"Crazy," Elaine echoed.

"Everyone knew Chrissandra was in line for it," Mandy continued.

Elaine nodded. "And deserved it."

I made an appropriately tortured face.

"No matter," Chrissandra declared. "It's in the bag for me next year. And it gives me more time to concentrate on other things now."

Like what, the continued destruction of my junior year?

"Anyway," she went on and touched my arm, "nothing personal about your locker. You know we're behind you finding your true love. It's just if we acted like it was okay for you to date a nonentity, it would look like we'd go there, too."

Mandy nodded.

Elaine did an "Uh-huh."

I scanned their faces. Who *were* these girls?

"Just know," Chrissandra went on, and gave me an air kiss, "that we couldn't be happier for you, Parker."

"Thanks," I said, and tried to summon one more smile, but I found my well dry. "Yeah, it's a great time in my life."

Motivation: Information can be imparted through your kiss, from your level of interest to your full intentions.

I glimpsed Tristan a couple of times that afternoon as he passed in crowds. A true-blue girlfriend would have shouted his name or shouldered her way toward him. But as an impostor (and one who had already had enough drama for one day, thankyouverymuch), I went with the head-in-the-sand routine and was relieved that he let me get away with it.

But on the field later, suited up to lead some defense drills, I'd have to have been Helen Keller not to notice the arrival of my faux beau. For suddenly, there he was on the sidelines, looking big and solid and pretty danged cute in darkish jeans and his gray "DeGroot High School Water Polo" T-shirt.

The action around me all but stopped, the gazes of a dozen and a half players racing from Tristan to me and then each other.

"Parker, isn't that your new guy?" Lyric asked, wiping her brow of running-induced sweat.

"He's *hot*," one of the froshies said, and was immediately seconded by her drill partner.

"Didn't he go to Greenfield with us?" another one asked, referring to the middle school.

"Yeah," a third girl said, and let out a dreamy sigh, "but he's grown up . . . a lot."

Emotions battled inside me. Embarrassment, reluctance and—to my surprise—a hint of pride. "Uh-huh," I said, in agreement with them all.

Lyric looked straight at me. Pretty in-your-face for a girl who it was easy to forget existed. "Aren't you going to go see what he wants?"

Her suggestion rocked me like a penalty kick to my head. It hadn't occurred to me that Tristan *wanted* anything; I guess I was getting used to him existing in the periphery of my life.

I walked over, eager to get him off the field, and stopped a few feet short of him. "Hey, you," I said, and reached back to tighten the band around my ponytail. I felt a bit dorky in my baggy practice clothes, and smoothing out my hair was at least proactive.

"Hey yourself."

"You need something?"

"Proof." He nodded toward some freshman-type people on an upper level of the bleachers. "My friends don't believe we're a couple."

I crossed my arms. "What, that kiss earlier wasn't good enough?"

"They thought you lost a bet, that a gorgeous older girl wouldn't fall for a guy like me."

I wanted to pause, to let that sentence drift lazily through the air for all to hear . . . but since no one who really mattered was on the field at the moment, what was the point? "Sounds like you've got smarter friends than I gave you credit for."

"Yeah, well, we gotta straighten this out if you want to keep *your* friends fooled. So now that we've had this wonderful and very public conversation," he said, bending down toward me, "I'm going to kiss you goodbye."

"You are, huh?" Energy fizzled inside me, although—believe me—I tried to hide it. "The See-You-Later Kiss?"

"No, the Official Goodbye Kiss. Shorter, but you'll still like it."

He was close now. Super-close. So close I could breathe him in, all male and clean.

"We'll see—" I said in teasing singsong. I started to say "about that," but his kiss took the words right out of my mouth.

Tristan was right about the kiss. It was quick, just a brush of the lips, with maybe a second or two of contact before the pullback. As far as passion went, it was low—maybe a three on a scale of ten (and I suspected we'd gone as high as eight or nine with the Leave-Them-Wanting-More Kiss).

Still, I liked it. I liked it a lot. . . .

Hartley, however, had a different take. (Surprise, surprise.) Her voice carried across the field, shouting my name—"Parrrrr-kerrrrr!"—with the demand *"Get back to work!"*

"I'm very important," I deadpanned to him.

"I can see that."

"They can't survive without me."

"And they shouldn't have to."

As I took a few steps backward, my gaze stayed locked with his. "Let me know if you need anything else."

A smile crept over his face, and I had no doubt he would.

Practice resumed. Some of the girls were actually good, and not just the ones who'd played on JV last year. I saw some raw talent—players with speed, with tireless legs, and some who could use their heads to make judgments as well as move the ball. With enough work, I figured they could be league-title contenders.

I just didn't plan to be around to help make it happen.

"Game speed!" I yelled at a couple of the slower girls (Smurfs, as Chrissandra would have called them).

But once we divided into teams for scrimmages, the play started to get good, started to feel real. For the first time since the summer practices, I went to that hot, sweaty, stinky place where I didn't care if I was hot, sweaty and stinky, as long as my side was winning.

And, as corny as it sounds, I felt like myself again. Focused, in the zone. I realized that I'd missed playing, that it was an outlet for me. And that quitting for the sake of saving face would have been just plain stupid.

"Up the line!" Hartley shouted as an orange-haired newbie tossed a throw-in. A short, squat girl named Dayle trapped the ball with the side of her foot and slammed it forward to me. I rushed it, did a fast receive, then booted it past the goalie to put our team ahead.

My team cheered (and so did I). Sure, it was only a JV scrimmage, but some days you had to take what you could get.

I think I was still smiling when I spotted Tristan back on the sideline. I had no idea what he wanted, but no way could I break ranks and go to him, so I had to hope he was enjoying the show.

Energized and positive, I watched the redhead knock a through ball between two defenders, straight at me. Receiving the ball, I heard her yell "Man on!" at me, letting me know the opposition was hot on my tail. I jammed around behind the ball and wound my leg back for the soccer equivalent of the football Hail Mary, then connected with force and, to my relief, amazing aim.

"Way to go!" the redhead cheered, celebrating my second goal.

I nodded her way, then threw a look at the bench for a silent *nah-nah nah-nah nah* at Heartless, an in-your-face reminder that I was one *heck* of a player (and that she'd made a terrible mistake). But Hartley's attention was focused down the foul line.

On Tristan. Who was now sandwiched between two ninth graders, Emma and Marg. They'd been taking breathers on the bench—and had apparently decided that this breather would include Tristan. His arms were crossed over his chest, doing that pumped-up biceps thing (which they were *so* falling for). Marg was grinning at him madly, and Emma was talking with cartoon-like animation, her hand on his wrist.

"Parker," Hartley boomed, calling me out for replacement, "will you go do something about your *boy*friend? He's distracting the players."

I felt heat race to my already mottled face, unsure if it was perverse jealousy that my non-boyfriend was flirting with girls his own grade or if I'd picked up a Chrissandra-type age-discrimination razz in Hartley's tone.

Nodding at her, I stomped toward the three of them, still very much in game mode. Coming to a halt, I reached out and plucked Emma's hand off Tristan's skin while tilting my head and squinting at Marg in a glare my dad and Tristan's would have envied.

"Mine," I told them, in my most mature five-year-old voice. "Now, you two, back on the bench." I waited until they stepped away. "And you," I said, turning to Tristan, "Coach wants you out of here."

"No problem, I was just—"

"Tristan," I said, shaking my head, "you're making trouble."

"I just wanted—"

My hand went to my hip, but I left the bite out of my

tone. "You're just too good-looking. You're killing our concentration."

"Your coach said that?"

"No, I did. Now go—and don't come back."

He gave me a long, slow smile, then walked away. I hustled back to the bench, putting my glare back on for the two froshie Smurfs.

"Um, Parker," Emma said when I plopped down beside her, "what's your favorite color?"

I opened my mouth to tell her to shut hers and watch the scrimmage (which would have sounded alarmingly like Hartley) when her friend Marg whacked her.

"Nice, Emma. Real smooth."

"Well?" Emma replied. "Jeez, I don't know how to do these things."

I let my stare bounce from one face to the other as I put the pieces together. "Tristan called you over to ask my favorite color?"

"Yeah," Emma said. "Something about flowers."

Marg rolled her eyes. "God! I'm not telling you any secrets, Emma."

While the two of them bickered, my brain was trying to get around Tristan's request. Flowers! He was taking things *way* too seriously.

But Heartless was summoning me over with a crook of her finger, so I knew this was a subject for another time. "Focus on the field," I told the girls, then jogged over to join the coach.

"He gone, Parker?" Hartley asked. She stood alone

down on the sideline, a whistle the only adornment on her maroon sweat suit.

I nodded.

"For good?"

I shrugged. "I guess."

"Okay. Thanks for taking care of that." Her gaze went back to the field—Dayle was on a breakaway—but she kept her voice full and directed at me. "You're doing a good job with the team. The players like you, already look up to you. I can see it's going to be a much better season."

Much better? For her, maybe. She wasn't varsity material trapped in a junior-varsity uniform. Besides, I wasn't sure what she even meant. We'd finished in the top tier last year and had had a heck of a lot of fun getting there.

"You might want to spend one-on-one time with some of the girls, boost their skills and confidence a little." Staring at the field, she let out a wounded groan. I followed her gaze, to see Dayle falling on her butt. "Get back in there, Parker," she told me, "and show them how it's done."

I adjusted a shin guard and scurried off. Not because I felt like being obedient or earning more praise from Heartless. But because I loved soccer. And because I totally related to the girl with her butt in the grass, waiting for someone to offer a hand, pull her up and give her a break.

I was waiting, too.

Nuzzling: As the perfect precursor to the perfect kiss, rub your face against his neck.

That night, I spotted Tristan out front, shooting hoops against a twilit sky.

A smile grazed his mouth as I crossed the street and headed toward him. He tossed me the ball. I caught it, aimed at the basket and shot. The ball bounced off the backboard, then thumped down on the pavement.

"Not bad," he said.

"Not good, either." I got my own rebound, then attempted to bounce the basketball from one thigh to the other, as I'd been doing with soccer balls since forever. But the weight and buoyancy of the ball was too different, so I gave up and tossed it back to him.

"So hey," I said, "I hear I'm supposed to tell you my favorite color. Something to do with flowers?"

He cradled the ball in the crook of his arm and met my eye. "Someone's got a big mouth."

"Apparently Emma's not real good at secrets."

"Apparently."

I waited for him to elaborate. When he didn't, I sat down on the curb and lifted my chin up at him.

"Tristan, you don't need to buy me flowers. In fact, don't waste a penny on me, okay? I think a kiss now and then at school is enough to keep everyone believing."

"I'm not buying you flowers. And I don't really care what your favorite color is. It was just something to say. A way to chat up the girls." He moved the ball over his head and lined it up to shoot. "Very soon this thing between us will be over, and it doesn't hurt for me to get to meet as many girls as I can now, while I have the opportunity."

He fired off the shot. I didn't bother to watch where it went. I was too busy smacking my leg (and wishing it were his head). I knew I should be relieved that he had such a good handle on the limitations of our so-called relationship, but the *last* thing I wanted was him making time with other girls on my dime.

"You're using me to meet girls?"

"Not 'using' . . ."

I jumped to my feet. "Hey, bad enough I'm dating a freshman. But one who's hitting on girls behind my back? Now the only way I'll save face is by murdering you in your sleep."

He retrieved the rolling ball, then walked toward me in long, even strides. "You're reading too much into this, Parker. Don't you realize that no girl would take me seriously right now? That she'd know that if I didn't realize how the gods had smiled on me by giving me you, I was not worth having?"

Huh? Man, was he good at double-talk.

"And not just because you're two grades ahead. But because you're totally beautiful and way out of my league. Not to mention kind of fun when you let your guard down."

Beautiful?

"The thing is," he continued, "I know it's not in the stars for us. And I'm okay with that. But you can't blame a guy for looking out for himself. Trying to better himself." He turned and threw up a shot that swished. "Because that's what this is all about for you."

I opened my mouth to argue but couldn't quite find the words. Then I tried to frown, but I felt the touch of a smile oddly shining through. So I went for the rebound, passed it back to him and watched him shoot again.

Still sorta mad. But sorta not, too.

We shot hoops for a few more minutes, then scheduled a "lesson" for the next afternoon. I shuffled on home, feeling oddly excited.

As planned, the next day, Rachael met me at my locker before lunch. We zoomed off campus in her adorable two-door sports car, which stopped being so cute the fourth or fifth time we circled the Taco Bell lot in search of a double-wide parking space where no one could accidentally ding the bodywork.

Clearly, Rachael had some issues. Including waffling on her commitment to soccer. But, hey, turning Tilt-A-Whirl green with car sickness was still better than eating alone—and it could only help my social life to be seen out and about with an A-list senior.

Inside the Bell, we quickly discovered we had more in common than being team captains. We both ordered Baja Chalupas, were into mixing sodas for the perfect, personalized taste and had mutual heart attacks when Luke Anderson cruised through the door.

Rachael started gasping because, well, he's Luke and has that kind of effect on females. And I went scrambling for an oxygen mask because I knew the slip of a lip here in front of her could ruin *everything*.

"Hey, Parker," he called out, spotting me. He had the sloppy college-student look going on, flip-flops, long shorts, wrinkled T-shirt and uncombed hair. I wondered if he'd just gotten out of bed or if he'd yet to go there.

My neck suddenly stiff, I managed to nod.

He cruised up to our table, then did a first: leaned in to give me a cheek kiss. I felt my eyes go so wide, I could take in all of the restaurant in one blink, while Rachael made a strangled noise deep in her throat.

When he pulled his lips away, I searched to find my own voice. "What are you doing on this side of town?"

"Laundry. I couldn't find any clean socks this morning so decided a trip to Mom's was more important than my first two classes." His glance shifted to Rachael and he studied her face. "You're Dan the Man's girlfriend, right?"

"Ex," she said. "We broke up over the summer."

He made a *hmmm* noise that I was pretty sure meant he could care less. While Rachael turned heads at DHS, I knew from conversations between Luke and my brother that Luke's idea of heaven was one of the girls closer to his dorm room. High school girls who lived with their parents no longer had a chance.

"This is Rachael," I said, remembering my manners. I didn't bother introducing Luke. Her gasp when he walked in the door, and her moan when he kissed me, had told everyone that she knew who he was.

He waggled his brow, then slid his gaze back to me. "You working hard—doing those, uh, drills we talked about?"

Everything inside me tightened.

"Because, you know, Parker, when the game starts, you're going to need to deliver."

I felt like delivering a kick to his shin. *Shut up, already!* "Yes, Luke. Don't worry about me."

A slow smile tugged up one side of his mouth. "It's important that you prove yourself a clutch player, someone who can be counted on, who doesn't give a teammate the *kiss*-off when the heat is on."

Okay, that was it. Now I'd have to strangle him!

Rachael was no idiot; she was sure to put two and two together.

I wrung my hands in my lap. "Well, Luke, since you missed some classes, it sounds like *you're* the one who's got some studying to go do." I nodded toward the food line. *Like, go!*

He held my eyes; then his grin widened. "Yeah, I need to get going. But I'll see you soon, right?" Then he glanced at Rachael like he was adding a PS to a letter. "Uh, nice to meet you."

"Yeah." She watched him lope off and, without changing her gaze, directed her attention back to me. "Wow, Parker . . . how do you know him so well?"

"My brother." I grabbed my soda cup (three parts Pepsi, one part lemonade, for a perfect lemony-cola taste) and took a long drink, hoping the icy-cold liquid would chill me out.

Because omigod, how lame *was* Luke? I mean, he could take lessons on confidentiality and keeping it real from my freshman boyfriend.

Still, I had to remain cool around Rachel, so I swallowed and tried to control my breathing.

"If I'd known Luke Anderson was *that* into soccer," Rachael said, still looking after him, "I never would have quit last year. I would have gone to him for drill advice. And anything else he wanted to give."

She grinned, and I tried to. "But you were with Danny, right?" I asked innocently.

"Don't remind me," she said, crumpling her paper

chalupa wrapper into a ball. "I can't believe all the time I wasted on him. I was so sure we were soul mates, thought any sacrifice I made was an investment in our future. But all it got me was a year of staring at his feet sticking out from under his car and a let's-see-other-people speech after his grad night. *Ass.*" She shook her head.

"But now," she said, brightening, "I'm all about meeting new people. Especially guys. Which reminds me, I don't suppose Luke hangs out at your house on weekends or anything?"

"Not so much, now that he and my brother are in college." But no way was I slamming that door shut. "I'll keep you posted, though."

"You do that." She smiled, then leaned across the table toward me. "And I'll keep you posted on a couple varsity players who may not be making it through the season."

My heart sped up, in a new and better way, better than when I'd spotted the town hottie.

"You know AJ?" she asked. "Even though her doctor gave her the okay to play on that knee, she's limping when she thinks no one is looking. And everyone knows Jessie struggles with her grades. So stay sharp. You just might get the call to move up."

I did a slow nod of appreciation. But the truth was, I was hoping I already had the gears of that move-up in motion. The question would be who I'd replace. Before today, Rachael had been my first choice, but as I sat across from her over lunch, sharing "secrets" and Baja Chalupas, guilt was raising its ugly head. I didn't want it to be someone I knew, someone who could get hurt the same way I had.

Still, I had to hang tough. It was Heartless's decision, just as it had been her decision to slam the varsity roster shut without me on it.

At school, Rachael and I parted ways. I moved in sync with the after-lunch crowd, doing that look-straight-ahead thing where you don't look directly into anyone's face.

But my gaze sharpened when I spotted Becca at her locker.

"Hey . . . ," I said, stopping and tapping her on the shoulder.

She looked back, briefly met my gaze, then turned away.

Huh? My brain scrambled, but all I could think was that she'd heard about Tristan and me. But that didn't make a lot of sense. Becca wasn't like that—wasn't judgmental.

After an endless moment, she pivoted on one heel. "You're still here?"

Wow.

That's when I knew. It wasn't Tristan who'd changed things. It was Rachael. And more important, me. "Oh, Becca," I cried, my insides churning, "did you wait for me for lunch?"

Her nonreply spoke volumes.

"I thought we'd left it open"—my words tumbled out—"like, maybe we'd meet up, maybe not."

"You *thought*. Yeah, I'll bet you did."

My stomach hit rock bottom.

"About as much as you thought about me when we started school here. When suddenly you had all these super-cool soccer friends and no time for me." Her nostrils flared. "Sorry they up and dumped you now, Parker, but don't come knocking anymore on my door. I'm not a total fool."

And then she stormed off, leaving me alone in the bustling crowd.

Orbicularis Oris:

The muscle used to pucker the lips. Keep it in shape!

I hadn't *dumped* Becca, I mused while my teachers stood at their whiteboards and talked. We'd just gone our separate ways. Friends did that all the time and didn't hold grudges. It was natural selection or survival of the fittest or some sociological term. Right? I didn't have to feel bad about this.

Much.

The thing was, in my heart I knew that no amount of analyzing or rationalizing could change the fact that she was hurt. Soccer-cleats-on-flesh kind of hurt. And that *I* was the source of her pain. I had to do something, say something, to make things better. As soon as I figured out what.

After last bell, I headed toward the locker room, eager to change into my soccer baggies and blow off some tension on the field.

Passing the staircase, I didn't as much see Chrissandra and friends hovering in their favorite alcove as hear them. Elaine was talking about a party, and Chrissandra interrupted with the fun fact that that night would be her and Kyle's eight-month anniversary.

Whatever. I couldn't focus on what they were leaving me out of. It would only drive me crazy, and maybe on to the place where I got mad—really mad. So I went past them head down, trying not to look or listen (or feel).

"There's Parker," Mandy said, so distinctly that even my best efforts couldn't block her voice out.

Chrissandra piped up. "Where's she off to?"

"Practice," Elaine said.

"Nah, Meeting her baby boy." Chrissandra laughed. "She must want it baaaad."

The blood that had felt icy with guilt all afternoon sharply rose in temperature. Okay, I *got* that they claimed their disgust over Tristan was all an act, but come on, show's over, girls. They were supposed to be my friends, the people I could spill my guts to and still count on to love me. Not to talk about me, laugh about me, behind my back.

Why, they were no more my true friends than—

Oh, God. My heart skipped a beat. *Than I've been to Becca?*

Except I'd never actually purposefully been mean to Becca, so maybe she and I still had a chance. As for my varsity friends? I no longer knew. And I wasn't sure how much I cared.

Minutes later, I was face to face with Hartley, asking if I could slip out early from practice. I admitted that I had some fences to mend with a friend, and from her quick and compassionate nod, I figured she thought it was soccer related (and probably something she had started by keeping me on JV).

To repay her kindness, I gave special attention to Dayle and a couple of Smurfs, taking them to a corner of the field and running them through some exercises. Focusing on the finer details of the girls' footwork, I was able to spot their strengths and weaknesses—and, soon, to see some improvements.

Which was sort of startling, and even fun. I'd never given much thought to my teammates' abilities before, other than to what they could do on the field to win a game. It was interesting to look at the team as the sum of its parts and to see ratcheting up the muscle in one place could offset power in others, resulting in a stronger unit.

When Hartley blew a whistle and pointed at me, I knew I'd been dismissed. And that I'd better set my mind on what really mattered: what in the world to say to Becca.

On the Benvenutos' welcome mat later, my brain was still devoid of anything but "I'm sorry." Which I blurted out as soon as Becca opened the door.

She just stared at me, and I felt my breath catching in my chest. If I could take any behavior back, I would. But all I could do now was hope she'd forgive me.

"You're only here because Chrissandra won't speak to you anymore," she said, getting straight to the point.

"No, I'm here because I now understand what a terrible person I've been. Which, yeah, I probably wouldn't have realized if Chrissandra hadn't decided I was a loser. But in any case, I'm here because I'm sorry."

Her gaze bored into mine; then she stepped away. I fully expected the door to close in my face. But she backed into the entryway and shook her head at me. "Well, are you coming in or not?"

I breathed in sweet relief.

Over Oreos and milk at her kitchen table, I told the story of the past two years, how flattered I'd been that someone of Chrissandra's stature had made room for me in her world but how I'd honestly thought that she—Becca—had moved on to new friends, too.

"I did—eventually." But the flatness in her tone told a different story. "Only no one who meant all that much to me."

Ouch. For lack of a better response, I continued with my story, bringing her up to the posting of this year's team rosters and how Chrissandra and the girls were now keeping away from me "for my own good."

"Sounds like you're finally getting a taste of the Chrissandra Hickey the rest of us see," she said, and scraped some Oreo icing off her cookie with her bottom teeth.

I shrugged. How could I explain that I'd always kinda seen it but it wasn't until Chrissandra had basically red-carded me from her circle that I'd felt it and cared? That was so shallow I even had trouble admitting it to myself.

"And you know what they say," Becca went on. "What goes around comes around."

I remembered that very phrase thundering through my head the other day and knew she was the one who'd used it. For fair-weather friends.

Like I'd turned out to be.

"Eventually Chrissandra will get hers," she continued, seemingly oblivious to my internal cringing. "I just hope it's in the next couple of years so I'm around to see it."

I smiled and nodded while pondering the best way to earn her faith back—and to redeem myself.

What could be better than bringing her into the secret vault of what was truly happening? I was 99.9 percent sure I could trust her. But if she ratted me out and blew the Plan wide open? Well, I supposed I'd have to live with it. The way she'd lived with what I'd done to her. Fair was fair, right?

So I took a quick breath and told her what Clayton and Luke and I had put in motion. And how I'd "hired" Tristan to teach me how to kiss.

Her mouth curved into an oval. "So, the two of you, the big scandalous romance, it's all bogus?"

"As fake as CeeCee Stevens's boobs."

Becca's grin widened. "So now I don't have to go ahead with the intervention, getting your friends and family together to try to talk you out of throwing your life away?"

I rolled my eyes—which was way better than admitting that, at this point, she was basically my only friend, anyway. "You're off the hook."

She did an exaggerated wipe of her brow.

"And to be honest," I said, and glanced at her wall clock, "he and I have another lesson planned for today, before our parents get home. I think he's probably waiting."

"Then you'd better get going. Can't dis a froshie." Her eyes twinkled. "Just tell me. Are we on for lunch tomorrow?"

"You know it. Even if Prince Harry comes for me in a gilded carriage."

"Prince Harry? You're still into him?"

"Yeah. I may lose my way now and then, but deep down, I remain loyal to those I care about."

She looked hard into my eyes. I know she got my meaning. Then she walked me to the door, and for a second, we just sort of stood there awkwardly. Then I reached out to hug her. After a long moment, she squeezed back—in what I hoped had the makings of someday again being a BFF hug.

When I finally banged on Tristan's door, I was huffing from the brisk run.

"Come on," he said, whisking me inside. "My father will be home any minute. We'll have to make this fast."

" 'This'?"

"The Steam Kiss."

My brain circled back to that first day in the street, when he'd challenged me to define certain kisses. I'd secretly freaked when he'd said that the Steam Kiss had to be done indoors, envisioning something risqué. But because he hadn't overstepped any personal boundaries, even though I'd given him total permission to kiss me, and because this was apparently my afternoon to trust people, I decided to go with it. Plus, I was more than a little curious about this Steam Kiss. . . .

He led me into the kitchen, where rays of late-afternoon sun competed with yellow countertops. I spotted a kettle steaming on the range top, sitting half a foot away from a coffee mug and an ice-filled glass.

"What's your pleasure?" he asked, grabbing the glass and filling it with water. "Hot or cold?"

It took my brain a moment to process that this Steam Kiss was going to be scientifically literal. I shrugged.

He handed me the beaded water glass, then poured some boiling water into the mug. "I'll go with the hot," he said, a wisp of a smile touching his mouth. "And be the strong, manly man."

I laughed. "As opposed to the little runt that you usually are?"

He ignored that crack, took a careful sip, blew out some breath and went at the cup again. In turn, I slurped down some ice water—which was actually refreshing, after the run from Becca's house. I waited until he'd taken a third, then a fourth, sip and took another drink myself, and then, following his lead, leaned in for a kiss.

Our lips met and parted. His tongue felt hot against mine, in a startling, pleasure/pain kind of way, but before I could decide if I liked it or not, he pulled a few inches back.

"Huff out a breath," he told me.

We both did. A few times. But no steam appeared between us.

"Let's try it again," I said, more interested in resuming the tongue action than in what swirled in the air.

But the sound of a car pulling into the garage put the kibosh on that. Tristan slammed down his mug, grabbed my glass, then cupped my elbow and escorted me to the front door.

"To be continued," he said as he unlocked the dead bolt.

"Yeah, but what I don't get is the odds that Luke and I will have a boiling-hot drink and an icy one at the sports fair."

"Next to none."

"Then why are we messing with this?"

He pulled the door wide open, a smile in his dark, dark eyes. "Why not?"

Surprising myself, I stretched up and planted a kiss on his lips before rushing through the open door.

I came upon my mother at the kitchen table, wringing her hands. Or more specifically, wringing the letter in her hands.

"George Murphy has done it again," she said, lifting the letter over her head. "Reported us to the city."

I thought of our perfectly painted gutters, of how Dad used a precision edger on the lawn and bushes and swept the sidewalks pristine. "No way! What now?"

"The width of our driveway. Can you believe it? If it comes up too narrow, it'll cost us thousands in man-hours, masonry and repaving." She let her head fall into the arms she'd crossed on the table. "I don't know how much more of this I can take. I mean, it started so innocently—we really *were* over code with that wall, and we fixed it—but it's become the monster that won't die. The paperwork, the appointments, the expense—the added stress on your father."

Not to mention on her.

"I'm just sick about this," she said, and drew in a gurgle like she might burst into tears.

Seeing her about to lose it did paralyzing things to my insides, like in one of those dreams when you desperately want to run but you can't make your body move. I knew I had to do something, so I patted her shoulder. "Clayton will help. He'll find out how to file an injunction or something."

"He's nowhere near ready for anything like that."

"Well, we'll put our heads together and come up with something else, Mom."

But she just stared forlornly into space. Wasn't she supposed to get all jazzed up about mother-daughter solidarity?

"Well," I said, grasping at straws, "I could talk to Tristan." Ignoring the fact that his dad had scowled at me, yelled at Tristan for hanging out with me and—oh, yeah—called the city on us again.

Mom's face contorted into a pretty good scowl itself. "It seems to me you've been with that boy every evening, and things have only gotten worse."

Ouch.

But she wasn't saying anything that wasn't true. And maybe because I was already feeling vulnerable, or maybe because all the lying was catching up with me I felt my face grow hot. The embarrassed, guilty kind of hot. It was one thing to play up the relationship among people my own age, to pretend to be in love with Tristan. It was another to play it down with my mom, to act like he was still just the stupid kid across the street from us.

Because he wasn't. And I had a feeling that when all this was over—after a respectable, make-believe I-won't-speak-to-you period—we might actually acknowledge each other and maybe hang a little. I mean, let's be honest. He'd surprised me with his maturity and his sense of humor. And while I was readying myself for the "breakup," I didn't exactly feel ready to give the kid the boot.

"Parker, you all right? You looked flushed."

I let out a poor imitation of a laugh and dismissed her words with a wave of my hand. "I've been running around a lot today. In fact, I'd love to take a shower before dinner," I said, then made a fast break for the stairs. "Do I have time?"

Mom sighed. "Considering I'm too upset to cook? I'd say you have all the time in the world."

Partnership: It takes two
for a good kiss. Choose your partner wisely.

I took a long, hot shower, letting the water hammer my muscles. Then I toweled my hair dry quickly, threw on my comfy jeans, a tank top and sneakers and reluctantly made the trip back downstairs.

My dad was home. He'd loosened his tie and was now at the kitchen table, popping open a pizza box. I was pleased to see a heap of steaming cheese and veggies, but given my mom's wounded look and the frown dug into my dad's brow, I figured this meal would be less about having a pizza party and more about taking care of hunger.

I scarfed down a couple of slices; then I drifted to the front window to look for Tristan.

Only to get the shock of my life—Chrissandra marching up the walk.

Talk about timing. Before she could ring the bell and alert my parents to her arrival, I was at the door. "Hey," I forced out, along with a tentative smile.

"Hey yourself. You doing anything? You want to come for a drive?" she asked, jangling car keys. Like everything was same old, same old.

I resisted the urge to slam my head against the doorjamb to see if I was dreaming, then shouted a few words at my parents and followed her out. Bracing myself for a final death sentence. Or worse.

But when I got a good look at her face, it was all relaxed and controlled and, well, Chrissandra-like. After a long moment, she even smiled. Okay, *what* was up?

"So how's everything with Romeo?"

"Uh, great," I said. Because it was. If you overlooked technicalities like the whole thing being a ruse and a scam.

She playfully punched my arm. *Ouch.* "I'm totally jealous, you know. I mean, not that you're with *him*," she said, "but that you've found true love." She thumbed her keyless entry remote. The car lights flashed and doors unlocked with a click. "Not that Kyle isn't my everything. But sometimes I think he needs a bit of a wake-up call that I'm his."

She laughed, while I think I just stared and gaped. It

wasn't like her to admit that areas of her life needed work. She was all about being fantastic and making sure those around her knew it. Now I *really* wondered what was going on.

"But that's not what I'm here to talk to you about," she said as we both climbed into her red hatchback, a birthday present. "It's about soccer. We've got a . . . situation on varsity," she said, and put the car in reverse. "And Elaine, Mandy and I think you're the one to take care of it."

Tension electrified my legs and arms—it was like that fight-or-flight thing you hear about when people are on the verge of being attacked by a bear. But I knew staying cool around Chrissandra was essential. She could sense fear, and she'd eat you alive. "Oh?" I managed.

"Yeah, which is the reason we decorated your locker a second time and have been bad-mouthing you. It's a cover so no one will suspect we're working together."

"Working together?" I repeated. I had to hand it to them for creating camouflage so effective that even *I* couldn't see through it.

"It's about AJ," she went on, referring to the senior who'd had knee surgery. "I saw her pour some pills out of a prescription bottle before practice on Monday. And they weren't antibiotics or vitamins, if you get my drift."

We rounded a corner, to see the bridge's traffic gates rising. Figured. I always had to wait for trawlers and sailboats to clear the bridge, but everything about Chrissandra's life seemed perfectly timed.

"When AJ went to the water fountain to knock them back," she continued, "I got a look at the label. Vicodin. For pain. Which, of course," she said, and made an *el stupido* face, "is against school rules. And also tells us she's a disaster waiting to happen on the field, that her knee is *not* at full strength."

I didn't get what this had to do with me and quite frankly was a little afraid to ask.

"Mandy thought I should go to Hartley directly," Chrissandra pushed on, her tone loud to drown out the rhythmic *ka-thumps* of the tires against the bridge's metal seams. "But you know how Hartley sometimes gets weird about my help?"

Weird? Yeah. Especially when Chrissandra was telling her how to do her job.

"Plus, I can't risk making enemies with my teammates if somehow AJ worms her way out of this. So the perfect solution is for you to slip an anonymous note under Hartley's office door while varsity is on the field, telling her to check AJ's locker for painkillers."

"Me?"

"Yeah. No one would think twice about you being in the locker room. They'd just think you hadn't gone home yet or were maybe hanging around to talk to Hartley. It's perfect, see? All the varsity players are safe from suspicion, AJ gets nabbed, and then you can move up to take her place." She held up a hand as if waving a Fourth of July sparkler. "Am I good or what?"

I knew I was supposed to clap my hands and gush, to

act as if she'd arranged high tea for me with my beloved Prince Harry. But ever since she'd destroyed my life, I'd had trouble taking her at face value.

The thing was, though, if AJ really *was* popping pills for pain, she deserved to be exposed. She could hurt herself—and the team—with a game injury. And slipping a note under Heartless's door was a heck of a lot easier (and cheaper) than bribing her at the sports fair.

But was there more to this than met the eye?

And then there was the other thing, which I let slip. "Unless Hartley promotes Lyric instead."

"Lyric, Schmyric! Ever notice her mouth barely moves when she talks? And come on, you wipe up the soccer field with her."

"Maybe," I conceded, knowing Chrissandra valued confidence. "But I'm captain. And Hartley told me yesterday what a good job I'm doing. I don't think she'd want to lose me."

Chrissandra pulled into the Dairy Queen lot and idled the engine. I knew she wouldn't dream of eating there ("all fat and fart," she had long ago declared it), but she conceded that it was the unofficial center of town. "Okay," she said, "we'll make things sweeter. How about I talk to Rachael, and after you leave the note, we'll both go to Hartley, backing you to move up."

"Rachael?"

"Yeah, I have a major in with her."

Funny, I'd gotten the opposite impression from Rachael.

"And if that doesn't work, we'll get a petition going." She patted my hand, BFF that she was. "And if *that* doesn't work, we'll . . . we'll . . . all go on strike. Like in the cafeteria last winter, when all the workers walked out." She chuckled to herself. "And it's not like they can train and replace the varsity soccer team with scabs."

I studied her face, which looked totally hound-dog sincere. I wondered if she was really on my side or if she'd just gotten even better at BS'ing. In any case, I was tired of saying what she wanted to hear—of playing by the Chrissandra Rules—and for once, laid my cards on the table.

"Well, great," I told her. "I'd appreciate any help I can get. But why now? Why not help me a few weeks ago, when this whole thing began?"

Something flashed in her eyes. "Oh, we wanted to. We *did*. But . . . of course, moving you up meant kicking someone off. Player limits, remember."

"And you, Elaine and Mandy were afraid it would be one of you?" I said, hoping she picked up on the word I was screaming in my head: *Coward!*

Her back went ramrod straight. "More like we just weren't in power positions." She put the car in reverse and backed out. "Look, I understand you need a day or two to think it over. But I'm sure you'll do the right thing."

"Uh-huh," I said, knowing what I really needed was electroshock therapy, to erase all memory of how they'd treated me lately.

"Besides, we're not done publicly humiliating you yet," she said with a light laugh and an evil grin. "We have more ideas."

And gee, how could I deprive any of us of *that*?

Chrissandra drove me home, chatting amicably, as if she hadn't just threatened me. As she turned onto my street, my heart turned over at the sight of the tall silhouette up ahead. Leave it to Tristan to be shooting hoops until last light. (And, coincidentally, just when I truly needed a friend.)

I powered down the passenger window, but when Chrissandra came to a full stop in front of my house, I saw that the figure wasn't Tristan at all—but his father. And another body emerged from a shadow.

My dad.

I realized with a start that the two had been talking. And while I crossed my fingers that they were finally mending fences (so to speak), the fury on my dad's brow when he turned toward the headlights stole that fantasy.

Before I could get out of Chrissandra's car, he was at the door. He had a bottomless pit of material when it came to embarrassing behavior, and if he went off on the turf war in front of Chrissandra, I thought I just might have to take my own life.

"Parker Elizabeth! Were you kissing the Murphy boy?"

I froze. "Huh?" I said, so shocked by his question that Chrissandra and her threatening presence beside me took a total backseat.

"Murphy here says when he came in the back door this evening, he saw you at the front, kissing his son."

Oh, crap!

In a desperate measure, I denied it with an "Uh, no, Dad" but nodded my head at the same time.

"I knew this was no good. But your mom insisted you were just showing him around school."

Chrissandra spoke up. "She was teaching him how to drive."

"Drive?" Mr. Murphy looked from me to my dad, exploding with gale-force winds. "He's not *old enough* to drive yet."

"That's why they were practicing out of town," Chrissandra explained, in what sounded like a logical tone. "So they wouldn't get caught. Then one thing just led to another."

"What?" the dads said in unison—arguably the first time they'd ever come together on anything.

"Nothing," I said.

But Chrissandra's voice was louder. "Their being in love," she said, then smiled at me.

Oh, God!

"Dad," I said, cringing, "it's not really the way it sounds."

"It had better not be," Mr. Murphy muttered.

My father pivoted on one shoe until he was facing Murphy. "What do you mean by that?"

"Come on, Stanhope, do *you* want your daughter involved with my son?"

"Hell no, but he'd be lucky to have her."

"Well, your daughter would be lucky to have my son."

Chrissandra elbowed me, grinning so big I thought her face would split in half. "This is *so Romeo and Juliet*."

I wanted to give her an elbow right back. A sharp one in the head, for opening her big, fat mouth. But I also wanted to power the window back up and instruct her to drive me to the Canadian border, where I'd disappear into the wilds forever.

Instead, I went with the only choice that made sense. I opened the door and stepped out. "See you tomorrow," I said, like nothing horrible was happening.

"Yeah, sure. But remember, don't say hi to me or anything. Tonight did not happen."

I laughed. Because at this point, I was wishing for nothing more than for it to be true. Then I slammed her door and watched her pull away.

I walked slowly toward the Murphy house as the grown men argued like grade-school bullies.

"I'm going to get Tristan," I said, hoping one of them would stop griping long enough to hear me. "We need to explain what's really been going on," I added brightly, praying we'd be able to. Without too much emphasis on the kissing stuff. So that I didn't get shipped off to a convent, and Tristan to a military school.

Quixotic: Take the lead from Don Quixote: when it comes to a kiss, there's no such thing as being too romantic.

Tristan appeared at his front door with one hand holding his cell phone to his ear, the other up in a give-me-a-minute gesture. I sighed and shifted my weight impatiently until he finished with a "See you tomorrow."

I didn't care what he was up to—that was his own freshman business—but, for some reason, he felt the need to explain that he'd been talking about an English presentation.

Whatever.

"In case you didn't notice, our dads are having a showdown in the street," I told him. "And this time, it's about us."

He muttered something under his breath, followed me out and fell into step beside me. "Look, Parker, my dad saw us before. Kissing in the doorway. But I took care of it. I told him you'd lost a bet and had to kiss me."

"You could have called and let me know."

"I did. You were out."

"Oh." I had nothing to say to that. "Yeah, well, Chrissandra blew that cover for us, anyway, and now they think we're in love."

"In *love*?"

He quickened his footsteps, and I had to break into a half jog to keep up. And while I understood the urgency, it wasn't like a house was on fire or anything. And was it really so completely offensive and out of the question that we could have feelings for each other?

Under the circle of light, our dads had stepped closer, like one was daring the other to make the first move.

Tristan took a couple of long strides, then busted in between them. He was the only other person who understood this paternal humiliation, and at that moment, I felt closer to him than to anyone on the planet.

"Dad, Mr. Stanhope. This thing between Parker and me, it's not real. I'm just helping her get on the varsity soccer team. It's almost over; then we'll pretty much go back to the way we were before."

"Practically strangers," I said, lunging forward. "Well, I mean, *maybe* we'll still be friends. . . ."

Tristan ignored me. "She hatched some plan with Clayton and Luke, and it turned out she needed my help, too."

I nodded, like, *Yeah, what he said*.

My father's gaze bounced from Tristan's to mine. I made sure to nod. "This plan—it's not going to get you into any trouble at school?"

"Not at all. In fact, that's why it's going to work, because it's totally within school rules. Clayton's got all that covered."

A smile tugged at my father's mouth, and he aimed his next sentence at Mr. Murphy. "My son's planning to become a lawyer. Have I mentioned that before?"

"Only about a hundred times," Mr. Murphy snapped.

Dad turned to me. "How much longer till this whole thing is over?"

"Just a few days. Sports fair's on Tuesday, and we totally have to be broken up by then."

"And at no point will you quit playing soccer?"

"Right."

My father pressed his lips into a flat line. Then looked at Mr. Murphy. "I can live with it if you can."

Mr. Murphy glanced at his son. "What are you getting out of this?"

"Are you kidding?" Tristan laughed. "Uh . . . hanging with Parker? Status at school."

His dad considered this. "I guess." Then he draped an arm around Tristan's shoulder and steered him toward the house. "But this doesn't change anything between us, Stanhope!"

"I'm still going to own your ass!" my dad charged back.

Tristan threw me a weary smile that I returned, and I made my retreat back to my own house with my dad.

I couldn't wait to see Becca that next day and get her take on everything. Although as I waited for her by the grill truck, it was hard to miss the irony that the girl I'd pushed away so I could climb to greater social heights was now the one I turned to, to bring me back down to earth.

"Talk about living large, Parker," Becca said later, when we were finally eating after I'd spilled my life's building drama. "All *I* did last night was homework."

"Consider yourself lucky."

I glanced up, to see Kyle crossing in front of us, shooting a grin my way. I was sure that Chrissandra had told him the latest and that he was laughing both behind my back and in my face now. Normally I looked away from his kind of trouble, but today I couldn't resist lifting my hand and waving. Just to make him cringe.

He pretended not to see me. "He's such a jerk," I told Becca. "Staring. Smiling. Trying to rub salt in my wound."

"Oh, he wants something from you, all right," she said, and laughed. "But I promise you, it has nothing to do with salt." I must have looked as confused as I felt, because she rolled her eyes and continued. "Duh, Parker. He's totally into you. Can't you tell?"

"Kyle? Uh-uh. He's with Chrissandra. And that's just his smile, I mean, the way he looks."

"Yeah. At *you*."

In the back of my mind, I remembered what CeeCee had said. *Huh*. I idly wondered if Chrissandra had heard anything like this, too. But Becca pushed those thoughts away by asking more about Chrissandra's plan.

"So basically," she clarified, "she wants you to put a note under the door and run like the wind?"

"Pretty much."

"Wouldn't Hartley recognize your handwriting?"

"I suppose I could write it in block letters or type it out on the computer."

"Or you could always cut out letters from magazines, like in ransom notes in old TV movies. Be super-dramatic."

I nodded, but my thoughts had slipped back to Kyle. I wondered now if those rides he'd offered me last year had had some sort of deeper meaning.

And I realized that it wouldn't have mattered. Even though he might be able to pass for Colin Farrell's younger brother, the fact that he let Chrissandra call all the shots in their relationship said volumes about his character. The more I had gotten to know him, the less I would have liked him.

I went for the take-charge types, the guys who weren't afraid to take risks or put themselves out there. Okay, not that I'd actually gone out with that kind of guy, but once this varsity mess was over and I had time to think about dating, I'd do a much better job of choosing.

"*Parker?*" Becca said. "You're not considering writing the note, are you?"

I snapped back to the present. "No . . . not really. I mean, it would be wonderful if it worked. It would save Luke, Clayton and me time and hassle and save me money—and it would totally take care of who got kicked off the team. But . . . well, I guess I just don't trust Chrissandra to have my back."

"Yeah, unless you're okay with her stabbing it."

The end-of-lunch bell rang, and Becca and I wandered inside. She was telling me about a guy she'd dated from the supermarket, and I was just about to ask if they'd tried any of the kisses I was learning from Tristan when some strained female voices, and a rush of feet, broke me from my musing.

Maybe I was paranoid, but I couldn't help jumping to the thought that it had to do with me.

"My locker again?" I muttered to Becca. It had been disturbingly clean that morning, making me think the girls were busy working on something grander than wrapping paper and coupons.

But we were still several classrooms away, so either the girls were still at work and had placed lookouts, or they'd done such a bang-up job that word had already spread. Or both.

Becca craned her neck. "Look away. I'll check and try to break it to you gently."

I glanced off to the side—only to see my JV-soccer teammates Emma and Marg flanking my (big, strapping and incredibly accommodating) "boyfriend," wrapping him with rolls of toilet paper from the shoes up. Marg was on one knee, perfecting a tie-off midthigh, while Emma stood, moving around the waist of his white T-shirt.

Several froshie girls watched at a respectable

distance, enraptured by the whole process, their gazes flying between Tristan, Emma—and now me.

"Uh-oh," one girl muttered.

Emma turned, saw me and flinched. "Parker!"

"English presentation," Tristan said from his frozen stance. "Remember, I told you."

"You told me," I parroted. Because I didn't know what to say, because I didn't know what I felt. I mean, who *cared* what Emma and Marg and Tristan did in their classes? Not me.

"It's about a summer read," Emma told me. "With extra credit for props."

"Tristan is the prop," Marg volunteered, clearly thinking I was too dumb to do the math on that.

I kept my eyes on Emma, who was getting way, way, *way* too intimate with my faux beau's body parts. Which brought heat to my face and tension to my muscles. For while this public display might have been as innocent as they claimed, it didn't change the fact that "my" guy had given himself up to these girls. Which made me look like the fool who couldn't keep him happy.

"What book did you read?" I asked. *"Captain Underpants?"*

The peanut gallery cracked up. Beside me, Becca laughed, too.

"It was a book about King Tut," she said defensively.

"King Tut," I said, frowning madly, "was short." Then I cringed, wondering where I'd come up with that and why.

"I think it's more the point of someone pretending

145

to be Tut than the physical resemblance," Marg explained, somewhat slowly. Like I was an idiot.

Fury—rational or not—engulfed me. I turned and stormed off. I'd deal with Emma and Marg later . . . as their "drill sergeant" on the soccer field. And Tristan . . . uh, Tristan . . . I'd have a good, long talk with him later, too. He'd have to know that he'd never make the A list if he let girls humiliate him in public.

"Slow down, Cleopatra," Becca said, grabbing my arm.

I did, working to catch my breath, too.

"What was all that? 'King Tut was short'?"

My face was still hot, but I didn't know if it was a wave of embarrassment or lingering anger. "I don't know. Emma and Marg get on my nerves—big-time."

"Especially when they have their hands on your boyfriend?"

"He's not—" But I caught myself. Anyone could hear us. I gave her a stern look. "I guess."

We paused in front of my locker. "Cradle Robber" had been written in red lipstick across the front, but I barely gave it a glance.

"You're jealous, Parker," Becca said.

But there was no twinkle, no smile, no nothing. Nothing but the truth, hanging out there bolder than the message on my locker. And I couldn't deny it. Not to Becca; not to myself.

Oh, God, did this mean I'd started to like Tristan for real?

My life was only getting crappier.

Reassurance: Show your partner how much you care. Try gently caressing his cheeks while kissing.

That evening, Tristan cruised out his front door, dribbling his trusty basketball. I knew this because I was peering out from behind our living room curtains. I felt like a TV title should flash across my face—*Stanhope Spies: The Next Generation*.

The thing was, I wanted to talk to Tristan about the way I'd acted at school, but I didn't know what to do. Apologize for freaking out when Emma and Marg had their hands all over him? Explain that he really shouldn't let girls—even cute ones—mess with his cool? Remind him that as long as we were "together," his actions reflected on me, too?

Nothing struck me as exactly doable, so I did just that: nothing. Including not moving away from the window.

Tristan got into a good rhythm with the ball, making a fair number of baskets, but he seemed to keep glancing my way. So when I saw him move the ball to the crook of his arm to leave, part of me felt relieved.

Until I realized he was headed in the opposite direction, away from his house.

I scurried outside to head him off on the lawn. My parents were in the TV room, and why tempt fate?

"Hey," he said, approaching, somehow seeming older and bigger and, okay, hotter than at any time before.

I returned the greeting, then dug my bare toes into the warm grass.

"It's our last weekend together, girlfriend o' mine," he said, and sort of smiled. The sky behind him was streaked with magenta and purple, and I suspected that if I looked around, I'd get a glimpse of the moon. "We should go out tomorrow night and get seen, give people something to talk about and remember."

He was totally right. But a flashy romantic date would mean lots of kissing and hand holding and snuggling and . . .

I shuddered inwardly. After what I'd seen in myself this afternoon, I did not think I could handle that kind of closeness without crossing some lines. What if I let out an involuntary moan when he reached for me, or my knees went and buckled from his kiss? How embarrassing would *that* be?

Luckily, Becca and I had talked about catching a

movie, so I was covered. "Yeah. Except I have plans with Becca. Why don't you do a friend thing, too? Then . . . maybe we could walk around Old Town on Saturday. There's a sale at Anna Banana's."

He slipped his hands in his pockets. "Shopping? You mean like being your errand boy between the racks and dressing rooms?"

Not a bad idea. In fact, I wanted to point out that being my personal servant would be a heckuva lot more dignified than letting froshies toiletpaper him—then thought better of it. "I meant that lots of girls will be there to see us."

"Likely story," he said, then grinned.

"Maybe we could cruise over to Maxim's, too. Because *someone* could use some new T-shirts."

"*Someone* likes his three T-shirts. Mr. Blue, Mr. White and Mr. Gray. Why mess with success?"

I rolled my eyes.

"Besides, Parker, what we need to do on Saturday is plan our breakup. You said you wanted a clean break by the sports fair."

He was right. We had to be dead-and-buried over by Tuesday. But I couldn't begin to go there yet. "We'll talk about it then."

I took a step back, intending to go inside. Only to discover he'd taken a longer one toward me. And then another, closing any gap between us. Without any effort now, I could touch him, inhale his scent, pretty much taste him. I was caught up in his aura, in his being. And was losing any sense of myself with lightning speed . . .

"Hey," he said playfully. "We haven't done the See-You-Later Kiss in a while."

Omigod, I loved that one, *loved* it. . . .

He angled his head, and I saw the hint of a smile. "We probably need more practice."

"But my—my parents," I said lamely. "Your dad . . ."

"We'll be fast," he said, his voice humming through me.

But the See-You-Later Kiss was anything but fast. That was part of its allure. Even when the kissers' lips eventually separated, it lived on (and on and on).

"I—I can't," I said, pushing him back quickly. "Not now."

He frowned, then shrugged, and before he could say anything, I hightailed it into my house, trying to block thoughts of Tristan and kissing and what I was missing.

My mom appeared in the hallway. Since I'd been forced to reveal truths about Tristan, the Plan and the kissing booth to my father, I'd gone ahead and told her last night, too. Including the part about kissing Luke, which seemed to mildly amuse her.

But from the tight look on her face, I suspected she'd been watching Tristan and me through the window in the door and was now less than amused.

"I was just coming to look for you, Parker. Chrissandra's called twice. She said it was urgent that you call back."

I thanked her, bristling. I really didn't want to think about Chrissandra and her anonymous-note thing. I was realizing that I had a more pressing issue to deal with: how to continue this sham of a relationship with my make-believe boyfriend without him—or anyone—realizing that the only pretending I was doing now was that I didn't like him.

I felt like I'd turned into a double agent.

Some kindhearted custodian must have wiped my locker surface clean, because when I arrived at school the next morning, the only thing staring back at me was a piece of paper jutting from my vent. My name was handwritten on the top and inside; the message had been typed.

```
Leave all books and personal items
in your locker and report to the
principal's office immediately.
```

It was signed by the office secretary and dated with today's date.

Since the only judgment-lacking thing I'd done this school year (so far) was date a freshman, I decided not to get *too* uptight about the ominous summons. And when I came around the bend to see a line snaking out of the office—made up entirely of JV soccer girls—I told myself this was certainly just something routine.

"What's up?" I asked Dayle, stepping in behind her.

"Handwriting samples. Apparently, an anonymous note was slipped under Coach's door, and we're all under suspicion."

Something jammed in my throat, and I suddenly really, really wished I'd called Chrissandra back. "When?"

"During varsity practice yesterday."

"What did the note say?"

She shook her head. "I don't know, but it couldn't have been good."

Well, duh!

My heart now pounding in every pulse point, I tried to reason through what might have happened. Clearly, Chrissandra had decided not to wait, to take matters into her own hands. But had she gotten someone from outside to do it? Or had she done it herself?

All that mattered was that it hadn't been me. I needed to figure out how to swallow normally again, and cruise on in there showing just a casual amount of curiosity.

Eventually, I was ushered into a conference room and told to take the chair facing the principal, Hartley and the lady I was pretty sure was the school psychologist. The principal explained that a player was on suspension pending an investigation, and Hartley added that this had been the result of an anonymous note. Then the shrink set off on ethics and how information sharing and coming clean on the tipster would benefit everyone.

Sure, everyone but whoever wrote the note.

But even if I'd wanted to be a rat, any information I had was secondhand. So I just shrugged a lot then, when they asked me to copy some sample sentences, happily agreed. I knew I was innocent.

On my way out, I saw that the varsity players had tagged on to the back of the line. Chrissandra's face jumped out at me like a beacon.

If there was something I needed to know, I wasn't missing my chance. "Chrissandra," I said, waving her out of line, "sorry I didn't call you back."

She just stared at me.

Oh, God. *Mistake*. What had I been thinking?

Finally, her lip curled up like she smelled something rotten. "Don't you have a boyfriend to go push on a park swing?"

Mandy joined the party. "Yeah, along with Bert and Ernie?"

Elaine opened her mouth, too, but her voice was washed out by the sudden rush of blood to my head. I could describe this only as rage. I knew I couldn't lose it with them, like I had with the froshies yesterday—not if I wanted my life back. But it took every single ounce of my willpower not to respond.

Besides, this was just an act, right?

I exhaled loudly, like their barbs had hit home. (Which they had—dang, double-agent stuff again. This was getting confusing.) Then I tossed my hair and called out "What*ever*!" and marched off.

I kept telling myself I was fine; but what was with the pressure behind my eyeballs, the feeling like I might burst into tears? Crying wouldn't exactly have been a bad thing for my cover, but it would have felt like bare-naked humiliation. Because I knew the tears would be one hundred percent real.

I was royally confused. I mean, the end of all this nonsense was finally here, right? Hartley would kick AJ off the team, and either she would move me up or the team members would revolt until she did. Chrissandra's Plan was in motion and actually working. And I wouldn't even have to deal with the sports fair.

So *what* was my problem?

Señora Trujillo took my hall pass and let me go to my seat without any questions or comments, And, although I usually found Spanish a nuisance, for once I was glad to conjugate verbs.

My peace was short-lived. When I cruised up to my locker just before lunch, two people were waiting for me: Becca and Rachael. And there was no way I could go off with Rachael in Becca's face—Becca had to be number one now—but Rachael's eyes were wide and insistent.

"We *have* to talk," Rachael told me.

I gave Becca a desperate look. "Can I catch up with you in a few minutes? Please? By the grill truck?"

Irritation flashed on her face (what, was today Emo Day at DHS?), but I think she could tell it was important, because she nodded and said, "I'll get in the line and order, but then you have ten minutes tops to get there before the cheeseburgers go cold."

"Thanks," I said, and hugged her, grateful for her trust and friendship again.

Then I threw my books into my locker and followed Rachael outside to an empty spot on the bleachers.

"You don't have to tell me if you're the one who wrote the note or not," Rachel began, crossing, then uncrossing her legs.

"I wasn't—"

"I don't care who did it. AJ shouldn't have been playing on painkillers, and I hope they give her the boot for good. But you need to know that Hartley thinks it was you."

"But it *wasn't*."

"Who was it?"

"I don't know."

"Chrissandra?"

Probably, but I didn't know for sure. I mean, if Rachael knew about AJ's knee, how many other people did? I couldn't afford to get myself in any deeper, so I shrugged and shook my head.

"Look, Parker, there's something else you need to know. I didn't just come back to soccer. Hartley came after me. She told me I'd go straight to captain, no questions asked, no cocaptain, if I'd play again."

I felt my eyes bug. "Great. But why?"

"To keep Chrissandra from taking over varsity, like she did JV. She said Chrissandra had bullied the other players, had argued with her coaching methods and had been a general pain in the ass."

Sure. But Hartley was an adult. And one with tough skin, at that. I'd had no idea how Chrissandra's antics had gotten to her.

"She's good on the field, but Hartley wanted to bury

her," she went on, "make her powerless. And to be perfectly honest, I have major issues with Chrissandra myself. So I was more than happy to come back and put her in her place. And believe me, next year, when I'm gone and there's no cocaptain to move up, you'll be the top runner for varsity captain."

"Hartley told you that?"

"She didn't have to. JV captains always move up—at least, the ones she likes. Just play your cards right now." She leaned in closer. "So if you wrote that note, fess up. If you didn't, be prepared to defend yourself."

"But I don't understand. Why does she think it was me?"

"Because someone—I don't know who—told her it was." Rachael stood and brushed off the seat of her pants. "Keep your guard up, Parker. Someone's out to destroy you."

I tried to nod, but the muscles in my neck had gone rock hard.

Soothing: Is your partner frazzled? Smooching is a medically recognized stress reliever.

Moving through the courtyard crowds to find Becca, I spotted Tristan leaning against a wall. Anxiety must have been leaking from my pores, because he took one look at me, said something to his buddies and beelined my way.

"Parker, you upset?" He fell into step with me.

"You could say that."

"Anything I can do?"

I glanced up into his dark blue eyes and considered blurting out all that had happened in the past few hours. Then my gaze zeroed in on his lips, and I realized that the last thing I wanted to use our mouths for was talking. . . .

"Uh-huh," I said, then grabbed his hand and pulled him into the building. I didn't care who saw.

I dragged him to Chrissandra's favorite alcove, under the stairs, which I figured would be empty at this hour. "What I could really use right now," I told him, "is that See-You-Later Kiss."

A smile sparked in his eyes. Then, no questions asked, his hand went to the back of my tensed-up neck, and he pulled me close. Closer. Closest. Until our lips were together, then our tongues, and our breath—even, I think, our heartbeats.

It was heaven not to talk, not to think. Not to be JV captain or the girl Chrissandra was supposed to hate or even Tristan's make-believe girlfriend. Inside that moment in time and space, I was just me, Parker Elizabeth Stanhope, throwing caution to the wind and losing myself in the arms of one heck of a guy.

"Omigod, you two," said a voice, cutting into my stream of consciousness. "Get a room!"

Tristan and I pulled back to see CeeCee Stevens making a fourth-grade gross-out face.

It was as good a time as any to part, so I broke free, only to feel oddly cool and empty.

"See you later," I told Tristan, then winked as I walked away.

He returned a goodbye that I didn't entirely catch, but I couldn't miss his tone, all deep and throaty.

I was no longer a walking bundle of nerves when I caught up to Becca. I gratefully accepted my cheeseburger, and in between bites, I unloaded all the dirt.

"Chrissandra," she responded with certainty when I was done. "She's the one who's trying to take you down."

I didn't argue but didn't agree, either. It just seemed too easy. She'd come to me privately about AJ and the pills. Why wouldn't she have come back for my answer?

When I got to my locker after lunch, a Baby Bottle Pop hung on a pink ribbon from my locker vent. I calmly untied it and threw it into my backpack. As long as the girls were still hassling me, they were still on my side. Weird as *that* sounded.

And who didn't like Baby Bottle Pops?

At practice, it was business as usual. We suited up and raced onto the field, with Heartless charging around, shouting out pointers and blowing her annoying whistle. I desperately wanted to talk to her—about the note, Chrissandra, my odds of moving up to varsity now that AJ was on suspension—but knew putting my head down and working hard was my best play.

I took my Smurfs over to a patch of grass to work on footwork again. I wanted Hartley to notice. And, well, I actually sort of liked working with them. I also couldn't help but wonder, if some older player had given *me* this kind of time and consideration when I'd started out, would I be a junior on JV?

My good intentions died a quick death when I cast

eyes on Emma (whose paw prints I still imagined all over Tristan). I cheerfully designated her our water girl of the day so that every time somebody's bottle got low, she had the honor of refilling it, necessitating a couple of long runs across the field to top off the cooler.

When she glared at me, with sweat beading along her hairline, I simply smiled. "Don't worry. I know how you like to go all out to please your teachers, and I'll make sure Coach Hartley gives you *extra credit*."

The resentment in her eyes deepened, to which I turned a Chrissandra-worthy cold shoulder. Then I charged off to set up a defense drill, secretly pleased that I'd learned a thing or two from my years at the feet of the Ice Queen.

Becca and I wandered over to the DQ after the movie. We ordered a hot fudge–brownie sundae, then dug in with two spoons, talking and joking around. No agenda, no talk of cals or carbs or fat or farts, no one to trash or kiss up to.

Later, a few players from the boys' varsity soccer team came over, and despite one of them asking me why I wasn't home babysitting my boyfriend, we had a good time.

Eventually, Becca and I decided to call it a night and hightailed it to my mom's SUV. As I headed for the exit, a car came in fast, straddling the line. I had to veer to keep from sideswiping it, and I turned to try to see who'd almost hit me. I wasn't surprised to see Kyle behind the wheel, his queen in her position of royal prominence beside him. They pretended not to see me, and I pretended it was because his inadequacy behind the wheel embarrassed him and not because they were too cool for us.

I dropped Becca off, then headed home. Turning into my street, I saw Tristan's long legs stretched out from the curb to the circle of streetlight. I wondered if he'd just gotten home from a night with friends, or had maybe shot hoops until he dropped with exhaustion.

I pulled into the garage and made the split-second decision to go say hi. I figured at this hour we'd be safe from prying parental eyes. But when I got to the bottom of the drive, he was standing, his head bobbing, suggesting that he was talking to someone. A five-alarm fire bell suddenly clanged in my head.

I skulked to a dark space on our lawn and waited with a bunch of chirping crickets. Until he took a step and a body appeared from behind him. A short blond body. Emma.

Crap, I should have killed her with push-ups and laps instead of just water duty!

I wanted to march over there. I wanted to run into my house, slam the door and pretend I'd never seen a thing. But most of all, I wanted to go grab my dad's cell phone to call the city to report the most heinous property eyesore of all: Tristan with another girl.

Thymely Kiss: Greek cooks sometimes use the herb thyme to electrify their meals—and their diners' kissing lips.

I crouched down in the dark on my front lawn, figuring I might as well get comfortable. But soon, Emma appeared in the glow of the streetlamp, pedaling a bike. Tristan stepped into the light as well, and watched her fade into the night.

I stood, needing no invitation to make my move. "*Nice*, Tristan!" I said when I got within shouting range. "Really nice!"

He looked my way, his brow furrowed.

"You *promised* me you'd wait."

He continued studying my face, then glanced in the

direction of Emma's retreat. "Oh, no, you've got it wrong. We talked mostly about our parents—hers don't exactly speak to each other, either—and then about you. How you play favorites on the team, and how she wants you to like her, too."

I huffed in frustration. "Right." I was *so* not going there. Dayle and the other girls wanted my help. What Emma wanted was my boyfriend. I screwed up my face. "Don't you think it's a little odd she came by on a Friday night?"

"Maybe. But she called first."

I eyed him harder. "Like that makes it any better?"

A smile tugged at his mouth. "Okay, *could* be she likes me."

"You think?"

"I *am* 'okay-looking'—or so I've been told."

"And modest," I added.

"Not to mention cool."

I gave him an exaggerated nod. In the distance, the bridge's bell clanged. "I believe the phrase is 'cool like that.'"

"So you can't blame Emma for feeling it."

"But I *can* blame her for trying to make a move on my so-called boyfriend." Without meaning to, my hands went to my waist in a take-no-prisoners stance. "I mean, like I said, you two can do whatever you want once we're over. Just don't make a fool of me now."

His hands mimicked mine and went to his mid-section, too. But instead of looking like a jerk, he somehow captured the sizzling Brandon Routh look in *Superman Returns.*

"I don't believe it," he said; then he took a deep breath and let out a laugh, more like the guy who played Superman in black-and-white on TV. "You're *jealous*."

"Jealous!" I repeated, for lack of a better response. Then I scoffed (which sounded more like a laugh, darn it) and thrust my chin out as if I was insulted. "Get real!"

He took a step closer, his smile widening. "You may not want me for yourself, but you don't want anyone else to have me, either."

"Oh, grow up!"

"What? You're no more mature than I am. In fact, if you could just get over our grade difference—"

I didn't know where he was going with this and decided I didn't want to. I jacked my voice up. "What—so we could be a couple for real? Maybe that's what *you* want!" I paused. When he didn't deliver a quick quip, I pushed on. "Well, you know what I want? A boyfriend who can drive. Or at least pick me up for homecoming and prom in a limo, not on his Big Wheels!"

I slashed that last sentence out like a sword, challenging him to a duel. But when all he did was stare into my eyes, the world went so quiet that I lost the distant ringing of the bridge's bell, the chirp of the crickets—everything. Everything but the sound of my heart.

"Parker, look," he said, ridiculously calm. "You can pick on me all you want, but all I've tried to do was help."

Wow. My face went shameful hot, like that of a kid who's brought home a bad report card. But before I could figure out what to say to redeem myself, he sighed and looked me in the eye.

"I guess this is as good a time as any to call it quits. I mean, here. Now."

What? No!

He flashed a sad smile. Which was more than I could have conjured up. I'm not even sure my shocked facial muscles could have responded to my brain's commands if they'd tried.

"What's that line," he went on, "about coming in like a lion and going out like a lamb? That'll be us."

"March," a voice said, and then I realized it was mine.

"March?"

"The lion-lamb thing." Leave it to me to remember clichés at a time like this. "Anyway, the kissing booth"— my voice tumbled out—"the lessons. You—you promised to help me," I added, again like some little kid.

"You're ready. More than ready. You'll spin Luke's head. Guaranteed."

Maybe. Maybe not. The truth was, I didn't care about Luke or varsity or Heartless or my old friends. For the moment, all I cared about was us. Tristan and me: partners, coconspirators, friends; even sort of more.

Did he want this thing over, for real *and* for fake?

My voice scratched as it worked its way out of me. "So, we're done?"

"We were going to break up later this weekend, anyway." He gazed into the night sky. I didn't know if he was looking for something or was just *not* looking at me.

"And besides, it's been . . . difficult these past couple days."

Oh. I swallowed. Hard.

Because of Emma.

He didn't have to say it. And how stupid was that? He could deny it all he wanted, but he really had ended up leaving me for her in the end.

It occurred to me to ask him to wait a few days before officially taking up with her. But considering I probably had to do the Big Smooch with Luke in four days anyway, I realized it didn't matter.

Nothing mattered. Except that I was down-to-the-bottom-of-my-soul disgusted with him.

But I'd been in deficit positions enough times on the soccer field. I knew how to wipe away the blood, hide the tears and carry on. Which in this case translated to a superior toss of my hair and a stormy exit.

Emma could *have* Tristan!

It wasn't until I hit my property line that I felt my insides start to crumble, when I realized that my position in the status-sphere had now sunk to subterranean depths.

I was a JV junior who had been dumped by a freshman *for* a freshman. And while it would seem that the only direction I had to go was up, I wasn't taking anything for granted anymore.

I was tempted to sleep the whole weekend, to keep a pillow between myself and the world. But if I'd learned anything from all this, it was that quitting was no solution. So I dragged myself out of bed, did enough sit-ups and tummy crunches to jump-start my brain and put in a call to Becca, asking her to meet me at Anna Banana's.

My mother let me have her debit card again. I wasn't sure if it was because I'd kept up my end by staying on JV, because I let her know I'd "broken up" with Tristan or simply because she hadn't gotten the last outrageous bill yet. I just took it and ran out of the house, knowing I was in need of some serious retail therapy.

At Anna Banana's, Becca and I agreed that Tristan's "in like a lion, out like a lamb" spiel wouldn't spin well with people. Nor would there be any mention of Emma. We needed drama—just not details.

And when we spotted my teammate Lyric Wolensky pawing through the cashmere-blend sweaters, we knew it was go time. Becca casually walked over and told her it was over between Tristan and me.

"Really?" Lyric said, looking up, interest in her eyes but her face barely moving, as usual. Sometimes I wondered if her family gene pool couldn't use a splash of cholorine to liven things up. "Something to do with that Emma girl?"

I hung back, pretending to look at necklaces, but I could hear everything. I realized I should probably give Lyric more lights-on credit—either that, or everybody already knew.

Becca covered nicely. "Nah," she said. "Parker just realized that the age difference would end up being the death of them, and, God knows, one Romeo and Juliet in history was enough."

I turned away so Lyric couldn't see or hear my stifled laugh. But while gossiping with Lyric was a good start, Becca and I both knew we had a long way to go.

The real talent rolled in some time later.

"Who's watching the baby?" Mandy asked, coming up behind me in a mirror while I modeled a plaid skirt.

I threw a thank-you up to the heavens, then turned, the skirt's lining making a silky swishing sound. "I wouldn't know," I said, and inhaled a noisy breath that I hoped had a soblike quality to it.

"Uh-oh," Elaine said, moving in. "Trouble in paradise?"

Becca cruised out of a dressing room and picked up my slack. "I think you could call this one paradise lost. Parker let Tristan go last night."

Elaine and Mandy sucked in their breath in surprise, then exchanged who-the-heck-is-this looks.

"You remember Becca," I said. "My BFF from middle school."

"Best, huh?" Mandy said.

"Who?" responded Elaine.

Mandy smirked. "So what you're saying is that she likes little boys, too?"

I met her smile and raised her one. "Actually, she just likes people for who they are. Whether they're dating guys who are three hundred and sixty-four days younger or don't have anyone special in their lives at all."

Mandy and Elaine exchanged "whatever" looks; then

Elaine turned back to me, her brow lowering. "So your romance is officially over, Park? Should I tell Chrissandra?"

"What do I care? Everyone's going to know soon enough anyway."

"Chrissandra will care. She cares about everything."

She cared about *knowing* everything first. So she could take ownership and take charge. What she didn't care about was my life or my feelings. But I just shrugged. "Then be my guest. And tell her I'm coping . . . as best I can. And hoping something comes along soon to help me take my mind off my pain."

"Something," Mandy said, "or some*one*?" Then she laughed, showing me how totally shallow she was.

Becca, on the other hand, stepped in and patted my shoulder. I touched her hand as if I appreciated the kind gesture.

Even if we were the biggest phonies on earth, in my heart of hearts, I really was broken up over how things had ended with Tristan. And Becca seemed to get that. And really *did* feel bad for me.

Wow, it was that double-agent thing again. Only now I'd dragged Becca into it. Soon we would need matching trench coats, sunglasses and fedoras, à la Carmen Sandiego. That—or years of therapy.

But right now what we had was two major rumor spreaders in the palms of our hands, a sale at Anna Banana's—and each other. And sometimes it was best to just shut up and go with what was working.

Ultimate Test: Kissing

is the greatest chemistry test of whether a couple is going to fuse—or explode.

Clayton and Luke dropped by on Sunday, mostly to raid the kitchen for food and the back patio for lounge chairs for some tailgating party, but then they spent a couple of minutes hassling me, caring guys that they were.

Luke wanted to know if I was ready for the kiss; Clayton wanted to be sure I was ready for the possible consequences. I considered telling them that I might not need them at all, that Hartley might weigh the evidence against AJ and simply give me her varsity position—but decided not to cloud their brains with remote possibilities.

"Yeah, yeah," I grumbled instead as I followed them out front to Clayton's car, carrying a couple of liters of orange soda. "Just be sure you know your parts, and we'll all be good."

I gave them each a hug and watched them jump in the car. With a toot of the horn, they drove off. Leaving me in the street—but not, as it turned out, alone.

"Everything still set for the sports fair?" asked the deep and all-too-familiar voice that invaded my space.

I hadn't seen Tristan for a day and a half. (Not that I was counting.) And I saw no reason to break that streak now. Still, my gaze raced to him with a mind of its own. He wore his blue T-shirt, the one that looked so good with his eyes. But as soon as I realized that I was silently complimenting him, that I was thinking of him in guy-guy terms (rather than guy-friend or guy-across-the-street terms), I gave myself a mental head slap.

Tristan wasn't important to me. I didn't need him, and I never would.

Except that . . . yeah, I kinda did. It was because of him that I would have the confidence to pucker up to Luke on Tuesday. And he'd given me some flashes of hope and happiness when none existed, not to mention some heart-stopping kisses. If he hadn't gone and replaced me, we'd probably have remained friends.

"Yeah," I simply said, both surprised and disappointed in myself that I didn't have a single snarky comeback. "We're on track."

He angled his head, probably to avoid the sun, and

his gaze arrowed into mine. "I'll be there. Watching and cheering you on."

Well, duh. He had to work the JV water polo booth, and of course, we'd both be keeping an eye on Emma in the JV soccer team's milk-bottle ring toss.

"Look," I said, changing the subject. "I saw some people yesterday, and I mentioned our so-called breakup." I rolled my eyes like it was just too silly. "And I might have made it sound like *I'd* broken up with *you*."

" 'Might have,' " he repeated.

"Could have."

A knowing smile touched his face.

"Is . . . that a problem or something?"

"Depends. What else did you say?"

"Nothing. What else was there to say?"

"Nothing," he agreed. "Okay. The important thing is, you're free now to kiss Luke, right?"

And that he was free to mack all over Emma. But again, it was not in my best interest to go there. So I forced a smile, told him I'd see him in school and walked off. Telling myself I was over it, and us, and him.

And that I'd basically say the same thing to anyone who brought up the breakup tomorrow. I knew that the more people I told, the better the chance that I would believe it, too.

If I was going to survive, I simply *had* to stay away from the front window and any eyefuls of Tristan that night. Logging in to IM up in my room, I also hoped to unveil the breakup news to a few more people. It seemed a lot easier to face the music through a computer screen.

After a while, Rachael came on.

u watching ur back like I sed?

My brain reeled. Instead of answering, I typed in my phone number and a big "CALL ME." Moments later, the phone rang. Eureka. I raced to my parents' room, grabbed their extension and plopped down on the carpet.

"Okay, here's the thing," I said, and blurted out what I probably should have told her before—that Chrissandra had approached me about AJ and the painkillers, had tried to get me to do the job. "So one way or another," I went on, "I'm sure she's behind this."

"Yeah," she said, then went silent. Long enough for me to wrap some hair around my finger. To pluck lint off my shirt. To imagine myself with a Chrissandra-thrown kitchen knife in my back.

"There's something I should tell you, too, Parker. But this stays between us." She drew in a big breath before continuing. "My junior year, when I didn't play? It wasn't only about spending more time with Danny. Chrissandra blackmailed me."

It was my turn to catch my breath.

"See, I'd been on the prom-decorations committee with her the year before. Danny and I weren't doing well, and I was pretty sure he was going to break up with me. One night, working late in the gym, I blurted it out to this guy Louie, who'd just been through a breakup. One thing led to another, and we started kissing in the hall. Chrissandra saw us and came up to me later with this whole I'm-going-to-tell-Danny thing—unless I dropped out of soccer."

Why was I not surprised? Rachael was older, faster on the field and more popular than Chrissandra. As long as she was around, Chrissandra would always be in her shadow.

"No way I was giving in, right? So I went to Danny, to break up with him. Only to have him tell me how much he loved me and how we were going to be together forever . . . and all this crap that melted my heart. So I said something about maybe not playing soccer the next year, and he thought it was a great idea. More time to be together before he left for college."

She sighed again. "So that was that. I didn't show up for tryouts, and Chrissandra got what she wanted."

"Until Hartley asked you back."

"Yeah, and by then, Danny and I were history. The jerk dumped me to play the college field, and I'm not talking sports. And soon I realized I missed soccer a lot more than I did him."

I sat up. "So you're telling me for sure it's Chrissandra who told Hartley about me?"

"I'm not. I honestly don't know. I'm just telling you not to trust her. And to know that she's capable of stuff you'd only expect to see on a soap opera."

A shiver ran through me.

My dreams that night were dark and disturbing. Who would have thought I'd actually welcome the morning light and the chance for real-life distractions at school?

But that didn't mean I was prepared to cruise up to my locker and find CeeCee pointing at a note protruding from the vent. I didn't know if I was being summoned to the principal's office for another interrogation or to a judge-and-jury trial of Chrissandra's calling—or worse.

"You see who left it?"

She shook her head.

Blowing out a sigh, I opened the note, to see bold, handwritten print:

Hi, Parker,
    If you don't have lunch plans, come to the courtyard. There's always room for you at our table.
                    Keegan, Rusty and Nick

"Keegan, Rusty . . . who?" I shook my head at CeeCee. "Courtyard? Did you see who left this?" I asked again.

A smile pulled at her mouth. "I didn't. But Lyric Wolensky's little brother is named Keegan. And I've never heard of another one."

I flinched as thoughts slapped together in my head. "Don't tell me. He's a freshman?"

"Just like all the other kids who hang out in the courtyard." She smirked. "I guess I'm not the only one who's heard that you and your man-child broke up."

I crumpled the note. "Guess not." I'd steeled myself

for snide comments and for heckling, but not for becoming the object of freshman fantasies.

I pretended to laugh it off, then turned to see my three former BFFs approaching. The one who cared about everyone and everything was occupying the center, of course.

"Hey, Park," Chrissandra said, without attitude, particular interest or malice. Her minions echoed her words, but all three kept on walking. Until soon I was staring at the backs of their heads.

"Aren't you going to say something back?" CeeCee asked, her tone lowered for intimacy. "You know, hi or something?"

I shook my head. They'd never even notice. Besides, this encounter wasn't about me. It was about setting limits on me. Letting me know I was worthy of a public greeting again (since I was no longer dating an inferior) but not conversation (since I was still on JV).

I knew the rules. I was ashamed to admit I'd been there when many of them were established, had condoned and obeyed them. But that felt so long ago . . . back when amicable public greetings had been a given. And before I'd realized that they weren't the make-lemonade-out-of-lemons kind of friends but rather the kind that held you down and made you suck on the lemon rind and choke on the seeds, "for your own good."

Watching them disappear, I could have sworn I had a sour lemon-drop aftertaste in my mouth.

As the morning went on, I heard a few chuckles

about the breakup, but mostly what I got was smiles from upperclassmen who seemed glad to have me "back with the grown-ups."

When Becca asked where I wanted to have lunch, I told her *anywhere* but the courtyard (and then explained about my new admirers). We settled on the grill truck again, and on our way back inside, we saw Tristan and a group of friends (but no Emma, I noted happily), and we all did a very satisfying and mature I-don't-see-you.

But I couldn't *not* see Emma on the field later. While Hartley explained how the practice would run late to make up for the one we'd miss for the next day's sports fair, I studied Emma's too-cute face and figure and dreamed up an announcement of my own.

"My footwork clinic is, as usual, on the far side of the field," I called out when Hartley finished. "And today, Emma is joining us, too."

"Me?" she said, throwing a heated look at me, and then at Coach. "But I don't need to work on my footwork!"

Hartley shrugged. "If Parker thinks so . . ."

As the team dispersed, I walked over to Emma and slipped a supportive arm around her shoulder. "I heard from our mutual friend that you're feeling left out. So I thought I'd include you so you'd feel like one of my favorites."

She pulled free. "I don't need help. I'll stick with the rest of the team."

"Fine."

"Fine?"

"Then you'll have the time to go to the equipment room and bring me some extra cones for the girls who *do* need my help."

She exhaled through her nose, and squinted like she was calling me some serious names in her head. Then she set off toward the building at a snail's pace.

Apparently, having a hot new boyfriend—and being able to hold that offensive steal over her team captain—wasn't enough to power her engines.

           ·

When the team hit the showers, Hartley called me into her office. I figured Emma had gone to her about me and quickly considered defense strategies. Deny any antifavoritism? Or tell Coach what Emma had done to so royally tick me off?

I settled into the plastic chair across from her desk.

"I'll be frank with you, Parker. It's come to my attention that you are the one who broke into AJ's locker."

I struggled to switch gears. Since she'd missed her obvious opportunity to confront me at practice last Friday, I'd gone with the hope that she'd dropped me from her list of suspects. But apparently not.

"You realize," she continued, "that even though nothing was taken from the locker, it's still considered breaking and entering?"

"Yes, but—"

"And that I consider slipping an anonymous note under my door to be a form of cowardice, not leadership?"

"Yes, which is why I'd never do either one." Well, okay, maybe I'd consider it, but I wouldn't do it. "And with all due respect, Coach, maybe you should suspect the person who is pointing a finger at me."

She bit on the inside of her cheek, nodding. "One last question: I don't suppose that little problem you needed to leave practice for last week had anything to do with all this?"

"No," I said, meeting her eyes.

"Fine, then." She rubbed her temple. "I just had to clear the air."

I nodded, wishing she'd clear the air with the blabber's name. And hopefully, get to the real point. Which was giving me AJ's position—right?

"You know how important you are to JV, Parker, and that I've come to rely on you."

My heart picked up speed. *Wait for it, wait for it. . . .*

"I'm excited about the way the team is coming together," she continued, "and optimistic about our standings this year."

I nodded, folding my hands in my lap, trying to look obedient and patient.

Only to see her stand. "Okay, then. I'm glad we had this little conversation."

Huh?

I searched her face, until her underlying meaning struck me as hard and fast as having seen my name on that last JV roster. Regardless of the opening that had just been created, Hartley had no intentions of moving me anywhere. She was happy with me on JV.

Crap.

That meant that the sports-fair plan was still a go. And that Clayton had better be ready with that fancy legalese. The kissing booth was my last shot at varsity this year.

Vacuum Kiss: When one

partner sucks all the air out of the other's

mouth.

The next morning, my brother called as I was heading out the door. He wanted to warn me that he and Luke might be a little late because of traffic. I pretended to be irritated, just because I knew it was expected, but the truth was, I was sort of numb about the sports fair. I hoped I wasn't making a gigantic mistake.

The day breezed by, and when Clayton and Luke's 12:45 arrival time came and went, I finished my shift at the JV ring-toss booth—where I only had to explain to three or four thousand people why I was still playing on an underclassman team, thankyouverymuch—handed the cash box to Lyric and met up with Becca for what I hoped looked like a casual stroll around the fair.

Oldies music blared through the propped-up speakers, songs about big girls not crying and *grease* being the word. We passed some sophomore guys emptying their pockets for kisses from Chrissandra, Mandy and Elaine at the kissing booth; saw Kyle and some friends wolfing down barbecued-pork sandwiches; watched Rachael shoot baskets to win a stuffed animal and checked out the cooking club's fudge-tasting booth. But no food tempted me, not even the slice of pepperoni pizza that Becca waved under my nose.

"I can't," I told her.

"Why? Nerves?"

"Breath."

She rolled her eyes.

"Okay, breath *and* nerves."

She rolled them again.

"Okay, nerves."

She patted my arm. "It's not too late, you know. To call the whole thing off."

"Why would I want to do that?"

"Maybe you don't want your old life back."

I watched her pop the pizza crust in her mouth, letting her words sink in. Well, yeah, no way I'd suck up to Chrissandra again. I didn't need her "protection." She wasn't the compassionate person she pretended to be to her close friends. In fact, I think the general population had her pegged better than I ever had. There would definitely be a change between us when I was on varsity. And that might not be an easy transition.

But I didn't want to freeze-frame right here, either. Stuck on JV, and with the knowledge that Emma's "boy-friend" was sure to come to every game.

I didn't want old. I didn't want new. What I wanted was better. And keeping with the Plan seemed like my only way there. As I watched my sophomore-year Spanish teacher on the dunk-tank plank, time pounded at me like a bad headache. Late was turning into later. And at some point, later would become too late. What would I do then?

So when a finger poked my shoulder, I felt my muscles relax. I turned. But instead of seeing the faces of my partners in crime, I saw a different kind of partner altogether.

"Don't you have a job to do?" Tristan asked.

Wearing his gray T-shirt and a smile that skimmed his lips, he had separated from his pack of friends, and the only person within earshot was Becca. I needed to close the gap between us good and fast—anyone could hear—but when I found myself senses first in his body space, I regretted the move. It felt like I'd lost too much oxygen, making me think of that Vacuum Kiss he'd talked about.

Breaking up, I decided, did not guarantee attraction immunity. Even when there was another girl in the picture. Even when you'd never really been together.

"They're just late," I managed, hoping that was, in fact, true.

"You need me to pinch-hit? Be his understudy?"

Wow. That would be totally wrong, but, still, I was touched.

"You're sweet," I told him. Noticing that he smelled good. Too good, and familiar. (Which, any way you looked at it, was not good.)

Anyway, I could not consider kissing him again, for real or for fake. And there was no way I could explain to him why he couldn't fill Luke's shoes. While he'd likely pull off the kiss better than any guy at school (or in Minnesota or the whole U.S. of A.), he just didn't have the clout of a former prom king. Or a pocketful of cash, for that matter. "But I'm sure they'll get here," I added.

"Yeah," he said, giving up without a fight. Making me wonder if he hadn't read between the lines after all.

But there was nothing I could do about that. Especially with Becca nudging me and pointing to the small crowd forming at the entry gate.

Which meant only one thing. Showtime.

My nerves tingled when I got a quick eyeful of my college cavalry entering the fair. I didn't bother to wave hello to Clayton and Luke, just grabbed Becca and hightailed it back toward the girls' soccer booths.

Mandy, Elaine and Chrissandra stood puckering and ready in the varsity booth, apparently in between customers. Lyric was running things at the JV ring toss along with a couple of midfielders. I noticed that Hartley had vacated her folding chair in the JV booth, and I didn't see her anywhere around.

"How are we doing, cashwise?" I asked Lyric.

"Good. Almost sixty bucks."

I nodded, then crossed the narrow alley and asked the same of Mandy.

"Why?" she countered.

I fought back a scowl. So much for the days of unconditional friendship. That had ended when Hartley changed the conditions. No, actually, my friendship with Mandy had ended when *Chrissandra* changed the conditions.

"Hartley," I said, with no compunction about lying to her, "told me to keep tabs."

"Okay, then. We've collected a little over a hundred."

Chrissandra trained her eyes on me. "Kyle's probably paid half of that—it's like he can't wait till Friday night, out at the lake." She laughed, and Mandy and Elaine did, too.

I was tempted to point out that I'd spent the last hour just a few feet away and all I'd seen Kyle get his mouth around was a pork sandwich. But why bother? It had to be happy on her planet.

To busy myself, I wandered back to the ring toss and bought a half dozen rings. I quickly learned that you had to *pay attention* to land those suckers on the milk bottles, and with the roar of voices and footsteps coming closer and closer, that wasn't an option for me.

I snuck a look at the kissing booth, to see Chrissandra

shoving Mandy and Elaine behind her, then doing a boob thrust and a welcoming smile. Clearly, Luke was approaching. And she knew a godly thing when she saw one.

"Hey, Luuuuuke," she said, drawing out his name as if they were old friends. (In her dreams.) "Kisses are three dollars apiece, but I'll offer you two for five."

Oh, puh-lease! All he'd have to do would be to look remotely interested, and she'd have one of her hangers-on start him a tab.

"Thanks," he said; then his voice increased in volume. "But I'm here for Parker."

"Parker?" Chrissandra echoed.

My name floating in the air, I turned their way. Luke looked the total part of a player, in a Hawaiian shirt, with his hair falling lazily into his eyes. People were starting to move in, drawn simply by his presence.

"You heard me," he said.

Chrissandra laughed in her "silly, silly you" way. "She can't work this booth. She didn't make varsity."

I cringed in case anyone glanced at me. It was pretty horrid to hear my loser status announced so loud and clear. And to think I'd choreographed and produced this degradation.

"Doesn't change a thing for me." Luke spoke his line boldly. "I'm here to kiss Parker, and I'm willing to pay plenty to make it happen."

My heart started beating all over my body. Anticipation? Excitement? No, I think just nerves again. But figuring it was about time for my formal entrance, I stepped forward and plastered on a smile. "Luke, hi."

His eyes smiled first, then his lips. (Boy, was he good.) "Hi yourself. You up for a kiss for a good cause?"

I nodded, while girls from close by wandered in and girls as far as five miles away drew a collective sigh.

Except for Chrissandra, who pounded a fist on the counter. Then she snapped a look at me—filled with anger and suspicion.

Making me realize a fatal flaw in our plan: Chrissandra knew there was nothing between Luke and me. No sparks, no chemistry. No nothing. She knew I was just a kid sister to him. She knew that something was up, that she was being trumped—or maybe worse. And she was not giving me one inch of Luke, of her status or of her power without a fight.

I narrowed my own eyes.

Hers turned cold and hard. Unforgiving.

I knew right then and there that Chrissandra Hickey hated me. Truly hated me. And that the hatred had been festering inside her for some time. The put-downs, the countering of compliments, the jokes at my expense? All meant to wound, to hurt, to destroy.

I just didn't know why.

Was this because of Kyle and his car-ride generosity? Or something deeper?

I held her eye, returning her "Die, witch" stare. Which gave her a jolt before her brow settled into something meaner and darker.

Coach Hartley pushed through the crowd, dunk-tank wet, in an oversized T-shirt and shorts over a one-piece. Behind her, I spotted a wary-eyed Tristan, arms folded, and the fuzzy crown of my brother's blond head.

"What's going on here?" she asked, adjusting the towel tied turban-style over her hair.

"Luke Anderson," Chrissandra announced, pointing at him, "wants to kiss Parker here at the booth."

Hartley stopped before him and leveled him with a gaze. "You'll have to wait a year."

Cords stretched in his throat as his voice rose. "I've got three hundred bucks that says the kiss happens now. All you have to do is put her on varsity for a few minutes."

Hartley screwed up her face. But there must have been at least a hint of temptation in her eyes, because Chrissandra jumped up on the booth's counter.

"Don't you get it, Coach Hartley? Parker's trying to *buy* her way onto varsity through her brother's buddy."

Crap! Was it too late to move to New Jersey, meet a family of mobsters and take out a contract on her?

"She's desperate," she screamed. "She'll try anything, since ratting AJ out didn't work."

Wisdom: The side you lean in on to kiss tells all. From the right you show your partner real emotion; from the left you reveal little-to-none.

Voices—mostly female—cried out.

Including one that sounded like Becca screaming, "Parker, I told you it was Chrissandra stabbing you in the back!"

And my own: "I had nothing to do with that, Coach!"

But only one person pushed her way forward. "No way. *Uh-uh.* You're not giving Parker my spot."

Chrissandra looked down from her lofty counter position with an icy glare. "Shut up, Lyric."

"I believed you, Chrissandra. I trusted you!"

"And if you just shut up," Chrissandra said, between clenched teeth, "everything will work out, okay?"

Hartley spun to look Lyric in the face. "It was you? Chrissandra talked you into breaking into AJ's locker?"

Lyric's face remained blank, but her voice betrayed her fear. "No, she only had me do the note."

The crowd made a tittering noise; then all that could be heard was breathing.

"It's not like I planted the pills or anything," Chrissandra said, and did one of her superior hair flips. "I mean, AJ totally deserved to be exposed."

Hartley's face inflamed. She shook a finger at Chrissandra, then swept it to point at Lyric. "Out! Both of you!"

Chrissandra's hands went to her hips and her eyes narrowed. She opened her mouth, then, for once in her stupid life, thought better of it and closed it. She stepped down from the counter and out the side door. There was no doubt she didn't consider this finished, but that would be her battle, for another time.

Hartley shook her head. Then, slowly, her eyes rose to meet Luke's. "The coach of the booth that makes the most money gets a reserved parking space all year."

I appreciated Luke's silence and the fact that the "duh" sounded only in my head.

"With both my teams collapsing," she continued, "I sure as heck need a break somewhere." She held out her palm.

Luke pulled the wad from his pocket. "So Parker's on varsity for the next two minutes?" he asked, holding it inches above her open palm.

Hartley grabbed the cash; then her gaze moved to mine. "You're on varsity for the next two years, if you want. I'm going to have to do some restructuring after losing all these players. And as much as I appreciated your leadership on JV, I need your game on varsity."

What? Huh? It was *that* easy? "I—I'm varsity?" I asked her.

"You're varsity. Although I might have you attend the JV practices as well for a week or so, until I get things on track."

"Done!" I said.

A smile burst onto my face, and I searched for Clayton in the crowd to send him a silent thank-you for his partnership and support. And then I turned toward Luke, who, I prayed, realized that even though we'd just "won," we were not done. We still had to do the kiss—and do it well—or Hartley might spot the deception and pull the team position away. She had to be sick to death of liars at this point.

I caught Luke's eyes and widened my own. For once, we must have been on the same wavelength, because he nodded, then yelled my name like a game-show host. "Parker Stanhope, come on down!"

I laughed, and skipped around to the side door of the booth. Mandy and Elaine flashed nervous grins, like they weren't quite sure where we all stood now. I didn't know, either. But what I did know was that they hadn't been there for me when I needed them. And right now, I didn't need them.

So fair was fair.

Luke stood waiting against the counter, his brows arched. If he was nervous about the audience, he didn't show it. Even with the hooting and catcalls, I didn't feel anxious, either. Maybe it was because I was so well prepared, or because the kiss was just a simple means to an end now. Or maybe it was because it was the first time this school year that all eyes had been on me in a good way.

But how ironic was it that this grandstand kiss would basically erase from people's minds my lapse in judgment with a freshman—and yet it was Tristan's teachings that gave me the skills and confidence to go face to face with Luke? Had my world done a total flip-flop or what?

As I moved closer to Luke, Tristan's face jumped out at me from the crowd. I wasn't surprised to catch him pushing forward to see the results of his blood, sweat and tears. But I couldn't say it made me happy to know he could watch with complete detachment, just a teacher proud of his student.

Clearly, none of our closeness or secret sharing had fazed him. He'd kept up his end by simply passing along his "craft." And now he was going to reap the rewards of a job well done.

Of course, I was the one taking home the grand prize—the return of the best elements of my life.

Luke leaned in and pressed his mouth against mine. I closed my eyes as if I were drifting away and listened to the whistles and foot stomping. The kiss was sweet.

Warm. And having him cup my cheeks with his hands was a very nice touch. But that was it. No chills, no shivers, no moans inside me fighting to break loose.

I wondered if I did have stage fright after all and just couldn't relax enough to enjoy it. Or if Luke couldn't perform at the same skill level as my high-school-freshman trainer. Or if Luke and I simply did not have chemistry together.

Or all of the above.

Or none of the above.

Because the ingredient that made the magic happen in my world was Tristan.

Wow.

Finally, Luke broke free, a smile engulfing his face. I put on my best smile, too, and added a very lazy and satisfied roll of my eyes.

The crowd exploded. Then Luke applauded me, I applauded him and we both did a little bow. Clayton came up and shook hands with both of us while I did a quick crowd scan for Tristan. Almost immediately, we were converged on by Rachael and a few seniors who were now my teammates. Hartley grinned at me like it was all no big deal, then headed back to the ring-toss booth.

"You are *so bad,* Parker!" Rachael said, giving me a hug. "Acting all cool about Luke, telling me he's just your brother's friend. Keeping him a secret."

I opened my mouth to explain, but she wagged a finger in my face.

"And using a freshman boyfriend as a cover. That

was priceless, Parker, priceless. People were so stunned that they never stopped to doubt you."

"Genius," a blond girl who I was pretty sure was named Victoria said. Several others nodded.

"Yeah, but—"

Rachael cut me off. "In with Parker, and out with the demon Chrissandra!"

More than one girl laughed.

"Welcome to varsity, Parker!" Victoria said. "We are going to keep you *so* busy with practices and games and afterparties that you'll barely remember that whole JV thing!"

Rachael looped her arm around my neck. "But don't worry. We'll give you sneak-away time with your steaming-hot boyfriend. As long as you bring him to parties and stuff so we can drool all over him."

"Rachael," I said, so strongly that the whole group finally stopped chattering, "Luke and I are *not* together."

She retracted her arm. "Well, you're still a heck of a lot closer to being his girlfriend than any of us here. Let us be jealous—please."

Victoria laughed. "And just don't tell us that fresh-man thing was for real."

I felt my throat closing up. It wasn't, of course. Except when certain elements had started to feel real to me.

Rachael joined in Victoria's laughter. "Seriously, then we'd have to send you back to JV."

I laughed, too. She was joking—right?

A couple of my new teammates fell back, and again, I looked around for Tristan. But in the opening, it was Becca who appeared, her mouth slanting down and arms hanging loosely at her side.

"Hey," I said, rushing up to her. "Wow, huh?"

But Becca just let out a weary sigh. "Don't worry about it, Parker, you're off the hook."

"Hook? Huh?"

"With me. You don't have to go slumming anymore. I get it that you have your popular, important friends back. And that there's no more need for me."

X Marks the Spot:

A mouth might form a perfect O, but X marks where the magic happens.

"No, Becca," I said, begging, gasping, freaking. "Please, don't do this."

People were moving away from the kissing booth now. The big show was over. But for those in the know (meaning me), the real drama was just beginning.

"Don't do *what*?" she drawled slowly, like each word was painful. "You're on varsity. It's what you wanted. I— I'm happy for you."

I didn't believe that for a second. "Look," I said, stepping in closer. "You're the best friend I could ever have. And you proved it by taking me back and sticking by me when nobody else would." I shifted my weight. "I'm going to play varsity because I love soccer and want to play against people who are great. But it won't change a thing between us."

"Until Rachael tells you otherwise."

I made a face. "She's not going to do that. And if she did, well, I've learned to stay away from people like that."

"You didn't ignore Chrissandra when she told you to drop me."

I paused, memories flying through my head. What? Chrissandra never said any such thing. Like Mandy and Elaine, she never even knew Becca existed. Chrissandra was just so cool during our first JV practices, I jumped at the chance to be part of the circle around her.

My flaw. My fault.

"What I did," I said, scrunching my face apologetically, "I did on my own. I moved on. I thought you had, too." When she didn't speak (and I thought my throat might close with regret and guilt), I added, "I'm really sorry. That's all I can say right now, and hopefully you'll stick by me and let me prove my friendship to you."

I could see doubt flashing in her eyes.

"I haven't given you any reason to distrust me since we talked at your house, right?"

"Well, no . . .".

"So believe me when I say I am your new-and-improved friend—who thinks before she acts."

A small smile tugged at her mouth. "New and improved?"

"Look, Becca, I've been the outcast and I've been the popular girl. Sure, popular was better. But you know, outcast wasn't so bad, either. Not with you by my side."

"Don't go getting all mushy on me, Parker," she said, and laughed.

"Friends?"

She let out a long sigh. "Yeah. Let's go toast that with some serious chocolate."

"Okay, just let me say goodbye," I said, and nodded toward my brother and Luke, who were chatting with some former teachers. "I'll catch up with you."

Clayton was engrossed in conversation, but Luke slipped away the moment I got close.

"Thank you so much," I said, and gave his arm a playful punch. We were *done* with lip locks.

"My pleasure," he said, then turned his back entirely on Clayton. "Hey, I don't know if it was those Starbursts or the cherry stems, but if that were an SAT exam, I'd give you the full eight hundred."

I laughed. "Thanks. I guess I'm a fast learner."

"I guess you are."

"Or I'm just cool like that."

Luke got called back into the conversation with Clayton. Leaving my words to echo in my ears.

Making me realize, *Right phrase, wrong hottie.* And also that Tristan had mysteriously disappeared.

I searched, but after another disappointing sweep of the fairgrounds, I came up empty. So with a heavy sigh, I went to find Becca.

Over a Tater Tot hot dish that night, I explained to my parents, in broad terms, that there had been a shake-up on the soccer teams and that I'd been moved up to varsity.

I expected congrats, and maybe the clinking of glasses. But instead, I got a nod out of my dad and a "That's nice, honey" from my mother.

"Come on," I said, my gaze bouncing between them. "This is what I've wanted. What I've been working for with Clayton and Luke." I almost added "and Tristan," but why rock the boat?

"Did you and Luke do that kiss in front of everyone?" my mom asked.

So much for keeping the waters calm. "Yeah, but I'd already been put on varsity by then, so it wasn't all that important."

My father's head jerked up. Fire lit his eyes. "You subjected this family to dealings with the Murphys for something you consider 'not all that important'?"

I tensed. Oh—I got it. This wasn't about me; it was about him. Him and Tristan's dad again.

"Your father," my mother said, her hand tightening around her glass, "consulted a lawyer today. Arbitration was suggested, a legal sit-down with Mr. Murphy and attorneys." She rubbed her thumb against her first two fingers, indicating the spending of big bucks.

"He also said we could sell the place and move," my dad grumbled, and shoveled some food into his mouth, probably to hold back some choice words about that idea.

I couldn't imagine moving—especially over something so ridiculous. I stared at my mother, the Tater Tots suddenly a lump in my stomach. "Maybe the sit-down isn't such a bad idea, if it's a one-time thing and gets all the problems out in the air?"

Dad looked up again. "Sure, and I can't wait until it comes out that my daughter has been using his two-years-younger son for *kissing* lessons."

"One year younger." My words slipped out, like somehow that made a difference.

My dad glared, and I didn't really blame him.

Struggling, I went for another tactic. "Well, Dad, it's sort of like a *Romeo and Juliet* thing. Even though the parents were enemies, that didn't mean the kids couldn't be together."

Something like horror creased my mother's brow, while a vein throbbed in my dad's neck.

"And look how well that turned out for their families, Parker Elizabeth!" He exhaled, loudly and noisily. "At this rate, we're going to end up broke and living out of our car."

I tried really hard not to roll my eyes.

"Honey, please," my mom said, touching his arm. "Your blood pressure. Worst case, we'll sell and move."

"I don't want another house. All the time and energy I put in around here, I've got this place damn near perfect. Besides, it's my home, my castle, my kingdom. . . ."

I'd seen my father go emo over Mr. Murphy plenty of times. But this was different. I was tempted to find him a hooded sweatshirt and an iPod and tell him to go chill.

When the doorbell rang, I leapt from my seat. And when I spotted Tristan through the beveled glass, holding a colorful bouquet of flowers, I slipped outside and closed the door as fast as possible.

"I had to guess at the kind you liked, and the color," he said.

It took me a moment to understand—to connect it back to that practice with Emma and Marg. My primary focus for the time being was to get Tristan away from my dad and my house. Now.

I grabbed the flowers, then his hand, and tugged him toward the street. "They're beautiful. But come on, my dad's home and this is no place to be if you want to live through the night."

Yummy: Kissing is an effective calorie burner, so go ahead and get an extra ice cream mix-in on your date.

As we headed out toward the harbor, it took me a few moments to realize that I was still holding Tristan's hand. And that I didn't want to let it go.

"Thanks so much for the flowers," I said, remembering myself and my manners. I dropped his hand to touch a petal in the lively mix of colors and varieties.

"I know you told me never to buy them, but I wanted to do something to celebrate you making varsity. And since I didn't know your favorites . . ."

"You got me one of each."

He exhaled a laugh. "Yeah, go with that."

We arrived at the grassy hill and settled onto the bench. It was the same place we'd sat just over a week ago, debating whether Chrissandra had seen us together in my mom's SUV. And while that seemed like a lifetime ago, I could still tap into that night and those feelings, how anxious and worried I'd felt. And now here we were, with all that behind us. Well, sort of. One thing I knew was that he deserved my thanks and my full attention, so I scooted closer, until my hip was practically against his. "Everything's been so crazy. I don't know if I thanked you for all you did. I never could have pulled it off without you."

"You're welcome, but sure you could have." He stretched his arm around the bench behind me. "You were an incredible kisser, Parker, better than any of those girls from camp, right from that first moment."

I turned and looked up, challenging him. "No way."

"Way," he said, and a grin touched his lips. "Nobody ever made me feel the way you do."

Now he was playing with me. I blew out a disgusted sigh. "Oh, come on. . . . What about Emma? When you kiss her . . ."

"I don't kiss her."

"Okay," I said, steadying myself, "but when you *do* . . ."

"I told you the other night, there's nothing between us. That hasn't changed and isn't going to."

Something lit inside me, and I felt the heat travel up my cheeks. Then suddenly, he was eyeing me with those dark, probing blues.

"Why all this Emma stuff, anyway?"

I shrugged, my shoulder bumping his. "Well, every time I turned around, you two were together . . . and then you broke it off with me—well, you know, *fake* broke it off—"

"Exactly."

I scrunched up my face. "Huh?"

"The whole thing was getting too confusing. The kicker," he said, and looked off at the harbor lights, "was the day you pulled me into the alcove. I thought you wanted to be with me for real. Then that girl showed up, and suddenly you're laughing and running off like we'd gotten caught. I realized it was all a scam to get seen. And I felt pretty stupid."

"No, no, not a scam," I said, touching his arm. "I didn't know anyone would find us. And I really *did* come to you for . . . relief. See, I'd read on the Web that kissing was a great way to kill stress. And I was freaking over stuff Rachael had said."

I smiled real big, hoping he'd buy in. But he kept looking straight ahead.

"But it wasn't about kissing *me,* Parker."

"Yeah," I managed, swallowing hard, knowing I owed him this much, "it *was*."

He turned toward me and met my eyes. "Are you into me?"

This was so awkward. Worse than awkward. Catastrophically awkward, terminally awkward, or a-phrase-that-has-not-yet-been-invented awkward. The deep-seated feelings trapped inside me belonged to the fake Tristan and Parker, not the Tristan and Parker facing each other on this bench.

But I just had to say what I'd suspected for a while and known for certain while kissing Luke. "Yeah, I am."

His arm inched forward, settling across my shoulder, comforting me.

Wow. What to do now, though? We existed in different worlds. He had his friends. And I was just getting mine back.

But maybe not if I admitted I was in love with a freshman.

Was that threat for real? And if so, how ironic was that? In order to keep what Tristan had helped me earn—varsity-level respect, on the field and off—I had to deny my feelings for him and walk away.

It wasn't fair.

Lost in thought, I lolled my head back against his arm. He tightened his hold around my neck, which only made things more confusing.

"You've become important to me," I said, knowing I had to at least try to explain. "I mean, I know I joke with you and call you Sparky and stuff, but that's sort of my way of keeping my distance. Since I knew this thing," I said, and wagged a finger between us, "could never really happen."

I willed him to nod, to agree. To make it easy. But it was no surprise when he simply arched a brow. Nothing about Tristan had ever been easy.

"Here's the thing," he said instead. "What if I was of a different race? Would that keep you from dating me?"

"Well, no . . ."

"A different religion? A citizen of another country?"

I shook my head.

"That would be discrimination, right?"

"Well, yeah . . ."

"And not dating me because I'm a freshman isn't?"

"I didn't say—"

He cut me off with a frown.

My shoulders slumped in his hold. He *so* had my number. "Look, Tristan, I promise I'll really talk you up in school, okay? You'll land an A-list ninth grader in no time."

"Give me a break! You're not getting this at all."

My heart seized up. Yeah, I was getting it. That was the problem. Like, Cupid's-bow-through-the-heart getting it.

"I 'broke up' with you the other day," he said, exhaling, "because I couldn't keep pretending not to care. And I was afraid if it went on any longer, I'd get all angry or jealous or *something*. And we'd end up as stupid as our fathers, mad-dogging each other from across the street."

A horn honked somewhere nearby, and a chill was settling into the evening air. But all I saw, all I felt, all I heard, was Tristan. I couldn't imagine him not being in my life, couldn't imagine not being able to turn to him, to talk to him.

To kiss him.

"So if we can't date, and we sure as heck don't want

to be enemies—friends is basically what's left. So, what," he said, and huffed out a sigh, "we shake hands and walk off?"

I shuddered, taking stock. I didn't know if that Victoria girl and Rachael had been for real about shunning me for dating a freshman. But if they had, maybe—just as Tristan had been showing me from the first day, when we swept up grass blades together—it was a matter of attitude. You act like you know what you're doing, like you're in complete control, and sooner or later, people start to believe it.

How else could I explain how I'd ended up taking kissing lessons from a guy just out of middle school? Maybe I was more of a fighter than I'd ever given myself credit for before. Maybe I was more than ready for this next challenge, as well.

"Shake hands and walk off?" I repeated, starting to come to my senses. "Yeah, we should totally do that. Except . . . not right now. And probably not any time tonight . . ."

"No?" A smile touched his face. "Tomorrow, then?"

"Maybe not tomorrow."

"This weekend?"

His smile must have been contagious, because suddenly, it was all over me. "Definitely not until the end."

"Or by the start of next week, for sure."

"Maybe. Or maybe we don't have to break up at all." I mean, if Rachael and Victoria gave me the cold shoulder because I'd found the right guy, who needed them?

"But in the meantime, I'm going to need a lot more of those See-You-Later Kisses."

"Not happening," he said, lowering his face to mine. "No more goodbyes. But I'm willing to give you all the This-Is-Just-Beginning Kisses you'll ever want."

I laughed, and his other arm came around me. Then his mouth settled over mine. In a perfect fit. In the sweetest kiss since, well, Westley kissed Buttercup or Romeo kissed Juliet. At least, to me.

Everything was wonderful. Peaceful. Perfect.

Until I looked up to see my parents and Tristan's dad marching toward us.

Zealous: Once you've got the guy who's right for you, kiss him like there's no tomorrow.

My father and Tristan's were almost a head taller than my mother, but as the three of them crossed the park lawn, it was my mom who seemed to be leading the crusade.

My first instinct was to jump from the bench and away from Tristan. I mean, no parents liked finding their daughter embroiled in an octopus embrace, let alone in the arms of the son of their archenemy.

But I realized that was pointless. If I was going to profess my feelings to my varsity soccer team, to the school—to the world—shouldn't I start with the people who loved me?

I untangled myself from Tristan and stood. A

moment later, I felt him beside me, his hands at his sides, too.

"Mom," I said, knowing from my years of soccer that the best offense is a good defense, "you need to listen to me. Tristan has been there for me—really there—lately. Don't judge us until you know the facts."

"And nobody makes me happier than Parker," Tristan said.

An "Awww . . ." sounded from somewhere deep inside me, and I turned to him with a smile. He grinned back—and I think we both lost a few seconds just looking at each other.

Then my dad cleared his throat. Bringing us back to the makeshift courtroom where I was about to be tried and found guilty of consorting with the enemy.

I met my dad's eyes. But oddly, the fire that normally raged over the mere mention of anything Murphy seemed to be simply smoldering.

"Parker," he said, "I'm not here to reprimand you. Your mother and I and George—"

George?

"—want to explain something," he continued. Then he glanced at my mother, as if handing her a microphone.

She took a breath that seemed to start at her gut. "I'm the one," she said. "The one who made that first call to the city."

The world spun before my eyes.

"I knew your dad was building the wall too high," she said, "and that in the long run, it would cause problems, especially when we went to sell. But he was under so much stress at work, and having such a good time build-ing it, I didn't want to shake things up at home by telling him he was over-the-top."

Over-the-top? *My* dad?

"So," my mother continued, "it seemed one anony-mous call to the city would take care of everything. He'd be forced to comply, and no one would be the wiser. And when he put the blame on George here, well, at first it seemed innocent enough. We barely knew the Murphys, and so what if Dad grumbled a little when he waved hello? But as you know, it soon turned ugly. And the big-ger it got, the more worried I felt about confessing, afraid a war of the same magnitude might break out in our marriage."

She ran a hand across her face. "But lately . . . well, despite what you've been saying, I've suspected you and Tristan had become more than friends. You kept slip-ping out with him. And those clothing bills! Something had to be up."

I flinched. Busted there.

"Seeing you leave with him tonight, I realized your father would never permit your relationship—for the wrong reasons."

Emotion seemed to catch in her throat. "It was bad enough, what my lies had done to your father, and to George. I couldn't have it spread to our children. So after you left, I broke down and told your dad the truth."

She shuddered until my dad's hand came to rest on her shoulder.

"After the shock wore off, I forgave her," my father

said. "To be honest, I was relieved to find a way to put an end to this whole thing. It was eating me up. So I suggested we go talk to George."

"And I can't say I minded an apology, or putting this thing to rest," Tristan's dad admitted. "And I understand about the lengths some people go to, to keep their marriages together. Sometimes I wished I'd done more of that myself."

My mother nestled back against my father, and he slipped both arms around her in a bear hug. (Which was a weird way to see your parents, but I guess since they found me in Tristan's arms, fair was fair.)

"So I'm hoping we can forget this whole thing," my mom said, "and get on with our lives."

Then, in a surreal moment, the three of them headed back across the lawn, as if riding off happily ever after into the sunset.

Tristan and I turned to each other.

"Did that just happen?" I asked.

"Man, who would have thought our dads would be so willing to make peace?"

He grabbed both my hands and planted a big one on my lips. Then we fell into step, bringing up the rear of the Stanhope-Murphy parade.

Nobody's life was perfect, and we still had mountains to climb. But so much of what we wanted was right here in our hands . . . so why not—for the first time since Hartley went all heartless on me—just relax and enjoy the feeling?

Now I Know My ABC's . . .

Even though a couple of weeks have passed since the Stanhopes and the Murphys essentially kissed and made up, it still feels like an out-of-body experience to wander outside on the weekend and see my dad and Mr. Murphy working side by side.

Today it involves handsaws and goggles on the side of our house, and, Tristan told me, up next is tackling some dry rot on their eaves. All this teamwork is gearing them up for making any driveway modifications the city demands. Though Mr. Murphy tried to call off the dogs, we learned that filing an ordinance complaint is like writing on cardboard with a Sharpie. No taking it back. So now they wait. Together.

Who would have thunk it?

Tristan and I have done some survivor bonding, too. We've weathered some looks and comments (mostly aimed at me), but all it took with Rachael was mentioning that with me "out of the way" she has a clearer path to Luke, and she gave her sanction to my romance. I don't think she cares at all who I date, as long as I keep up my end on the field. And being tight with the team captain can only be a good thing (as long as that captain isn't named Chrissandra Hickey).

Speaking of Chrissandra, she got her butt kicked off the team for good. Mandy and Elaine admitted that Chrissandra had major jealousy issues with me because she thought I was a threat to her popularity and love life. In fact, she apparently got close to Kyle last year by pretending to help him "hook" me—and then went in for the kill herself.

And she totally planned to rat me out to Hartley as the sole instigator behind the discovery of AJ's pills, which she figured would prevent me from ever making varsity and going against her for captain next year.

Look who got the last laugh.

Over on JV, Lyric got the boot, too. When Hartley asked who I recommended as the new captain, I swallowed my pride and told her Emma. I'd been rough on the girl, and for the most part, she didn't deserve it. Emma came to me later and thanked me, and I've been dropping by practices whenever I have free time, help-ing with drills.

Back on my own team, I only talk to Elaine and Mandy to be polite. I've learned who my real friends are. And number one in my life is Becca. She helped teach me a lot about popularity and loyalty—and, well, myself. And while she doesn't plan to date a freshman anytime soon, she's happy for me and how things have worked out with Tristan.

I'm happy, too. And looking forward to later this month, when our birthdays fall, one day apart. He's promised me something special called the Birthday Kiss. I'm hoping that there are no lit candles or noise-makers involved—but that it *is* one of those kisses that has to be done indoors. Maybe even behind *closed* doors?

There's so much more for us both to learn about kissing and falling in love and each other. But no rush. For now, we have all the time in the world.

Jari Blakely Kirkwood

Tina Ferraro refuses to talk about her first kisses (besides, do spin-the-bottle kisses really count?), but she's happy to share all about her books if you want to visit her Web site, www.tinaferraro.com. She lives with her husband and their three kids in Southern California. *The ABC's of Kissing Boys* is her third book for young readers.